Princess DisGrace

Winter Term at Tall Towers

Lou Kuenzler

Illustrated by Kimberley Scott

■SCHOLASTIC

Scholastic Children's Books
An imprint of Scholastic Ltd
Euston House, 24 Eversholt Street, London, NW1 1DB, UK
Registered office: Westfield Road, Southam, Warwickshire, CV47 0RA
SCHOLASTIC and associated logos are trademarks and/or
registered trademarks of Scholastic Inc.

First published in the UK by Scholastic Ltd, 2015

ISBN 978 1407 15258 5

A CIP catalogue record for this book
is available from the British Library.

Printed by CPI Group (UK) Ltd, Croydon, CR0 4YY
Papers used by Scholastic Children's Books are made
from wood grown in sustainable forests.

1 3 5 7 9 10 8 6 4 2

www.scholastic.co.uk

To Hans who's from a land
of ice and snow. -LK

CHAPTER ONE
Snow

One morning, halfway through the winter term, Princess Grace woke up to find she was lying on the floor.

"Not again!" she groaned, opening one eye. As usual, she had rolled over in the middle of the night and fallen out of bed. "It's freezing down here!" she said, shivering as she grabbed a blanket and wrapped it around her long skinny legs. Her big flat feet felt like frozen blocks of ice. For a moment, she thought she must be at home – back in Cragland, the cold mountain kingdom where she lived with Papa, her little sister Princess Pip and a hundred wild warriors with their herds of hairy yaks.

But as Grace blinked sleepily, she saw three soft white beds and knew at once that

she was in Sky Dorm, the pretty little school dormitory she shared with her two best friends, Princess Scarlet and Princess Izumi. Although the girls were now in the Second Year at Tall Towers Princess Academy, they had been allowed to keep the same high attic room they had shared last year.

"Brrr! I have never known it as cold as this on Coronet Island before," shuddered Grace, wriggling under the bed in search of her warm yak-hair slippers.

"It is chilly," agreed Princess Izumi, poking her small dark head over the top of her covers and shivering too.

"Freezing!" gasped Princess Scarlet, stretching like a ballet dancer as she stepped lightly out of bed and wrapped her pink silk dressing gown around her shoulders.

Grace had only managed to find one slipper and there was no sign of her dressing gown anywhere. She hopped across the freezing floor towards the window.

"If I didn't know any better," she said through chattering teeth, "I'd say there'd been— Wow!" Grace let out a whoop of delight as she pulled back the curtains. "*Snow!*" The world outside looked as soft and white as the blankets on their beds.

"Yippee! Now we're going to have some fun," Grace grinned.

"How beautiful!" Artistic Izumi joined her by the frosted window. Sky Dorm was at the very top of the Dormitory Tower, so they had a clear view across the whole of the snowy island, right down to the Sapphire Sea, which was sparkling icy blue against the frozen pearl-white shore. Even the yellow sand was sugary with snow.

"Isn't it magical?" said Scarlet, standing on tiptoes to peep over their heads. "It's like a winter wonderland."

"Come on," cried Grace, scrambling into her clothes. She grabbed the shaggy yak-hair coat she had stuffed at the very back of the wardrobe. "I never thought I'd need this at Tall Towers," she laughed. She wore the hairy winter coat nearly every day at home in Cragland, but it was better suited to one of Papa's wild warriors than a pupil at a royal school.

"This will keep me good and warm," Grace grinned. "I might not know much about being a proper princess, but I do know all about snow!"

Grace hurtled across the snowy lawn, dodging between groups of princesses who were admiring the wintry gardens and gathering pretty frosted berries in their baskets.

"Here goes!" she cried, flinging herself backwards on a thick, clear patch of snow. She swooshed her arms and legs to make the shape of wings.

"It looks like a snow fairy or an angel," said Izumi.

"At home, we call them snow bats," giggled Grace. She staggered to her feet and shook the snow from her enormous winter coat.

"My go!" said Izumi.

But Grace had other ideas. She couldn't believe the Tall Towers princesses were strolling so calmly along the snowy paths. Didn't anyone know how to have fun?

"How about a snowball fight?" she grinned, scooping up a handful of soft white powder and flinging it at her two best friends.

"Help!" Scarlet leapt sideways, but Izumi wasn't quite so quick. The snowball shot up the sleeve of her velvet cape.

"I'll get you for that!" she giggled, hurling a snowball back at Grace just as Scarlet threw one too.

Grace tried to duck but was hit from both sides. Laughing, she toppled over into the snow.

"Snowballs! How brilliant," cried Visalotta, the wealthiest princess in the whole school.

"I'm never allowed to do this at home." She tossed her white fur muffler high in the air and joined in the game, hurling big soft snowballs at Grace and her friends.

Before long, there was chaos in the garden. Princesses were leaping in every direction, snowballs and laughter flying through the frosty air.

Everyone was having fun. But, as usual, Grace's spiteful cousin, Princess Precious, threatened to spoil it all. Instead of throwing the soft powdery snow, she made a pile of small, hard, icy bullets.

"Got you!" she cried, hitting a tiny First Year princess in bright red boots.

"Stop that!" cried Grace. "Pick on someone your own size!"

Although Precious was in the Second Year now, like Grace and her friends, she was only throwing her sharp snowballs at the new

First Years. They had been at the school for just a few weeks and were either too small or too scared to fight back.

"You can't tell me what to do, Grace … or should I say Princess *Disgrace*?" sneered Precious, making another pellet of snow in her hand. "You're the worst princess in this whole school."

"Worst princess!" chorused the pink-faced twins Trinket and Truffle, who always followed Precious everywhere, copying everything she said.

Precious raised the next hard snowball and grinned.

"Look out!" Grace leapt forward and bundled three small First Years out of the way. Precious's sharp snowball went flying way over their heads as Grace knocked the tiny trio of girls flat in the snow. "Ooops! Sorry!"

"Don't worry! You were only trying to save us," said the little princess with the red boots. But before Grace could help the younger girls to their feet, a dark shadow fell across the snow. Fairy Godmother Flint, the strict First Year form teacher, was staring down at them.

"What is going on here?" she asked as the garden fell silent and the snowball fight came to an end. "This is a most un-princess like way to behave!"

Grace shrunk into the hood of her coat. One of the very best things about being in the Second Year was that Fairy Godmother Flint – or old Flintheart, as the girls called her – was no longer their form teacher. Instead, Fairy Godmother Webster, the sleepy school librarian, was in charge of their class. The only trouble was, Flintheart still seemed to be waiting round every corner – and every hedge – ready to catch Grace doing just the sort of things that a proper princess is never supposed to do.

"Excuse me, Fairy Godmother Flint," said Precious, raising her hand and speaking in her sweetest, most helpful voice. "I think

you ought to know that it was Princess
Grace who started the snowball fight."

CHAPTER TWO
The Frozen Lake

As a punishment for starting the snowball fight, Grace was sent to sit in the library and read three chapters of Flintheart's favourite textbook, *Princess Manners For Beginners* by B. Royal.

"It might give you some idea how a proper princess ought to behave," sighed Flintheart. "And you can go on your own!" she added sternly as Scarlet and Izumi started to follow Grace towards the library.

Grace had never actually read anything

from *Princess Manners For Beginners* before, though she had spent many hours trying to balance a copy of the book on her head during Flintheart's deportment classes last year.

"Let's see." She opened the contents page, hoping there might be something on rules for a winter princess that she could impress Flintheart with if there was a test. But although there were three chapters on proper curtsies and two on napkin folding, there didn't seem to be anything on how to behave in the snow.

Noticing that Fairy Godmother Webster had dozed off at her desk, Grace stood up and tiptoed to the window. She could see a V of white snow geese flying away from Coronet Island across the sea. "Have a good flight," she whispered. It was the same in Cragland – the geese always flew off as soon as the first snow came. They'd find somewhere warm to spend the winter and wouldn't come back until the spring.

"Goodness, are you still here, my dear?" said Fairy Godmother Webster, sitting up and blinking. "I'm sure old Flintheart – I mean Fairy Godmother Flint – wouldn't want you cooped up inside all day. Go on!" she smiled. "Get back out in the snow and enjoy yourself."

"Thank you." Grace leapt to her feet and tossed *Princess Manners For Beginners* back on to the shelf. The nearest thing she'd found to advice about winter was the correct way for a princess to eat a snow cone with a spoon.

"I don't suppose it'll be much fun outside, though," she sighed. "Not if we can't have snowball fights. And we won't be able to go riding in all this snow." She thought of

Billy, her beloved shaggy unicorn, tucked up in his stable. She would have to give him some warm honey mash later to keep away the winter chills.

"It wouldn't be safe to ride the unicorns in case they slip. And there had *definitely* better not be any more snowballs," agreed Fairy Godmother Webster. "But that doesn't mean you won't have fun. There hasn't been a winter like this on Coronet Island for years," she said wistfully. "But when it does get this cold, the Tall Towers princesses always go out on the ice."

"On the big lake?" asked Grace, thinking of the beautiful stretch of silvery water where the princesses rowed boats in summer.

"That's right," said Fairy Godmother Webster. "As long as the ice is thick enough and the teachers say it's safe."

"How exciting," cried Grace. "Thank you

for letting me go out!" She dashed to the door. If Flintheart had been in charge of the punishment, she'd have been here for hours yet.

"Keep warm and dress properly for the ice," murmured the fairy godmother, yawning and laying her head back down on the desk.

"Don't worry, I will," Grace promised, closing the door quietly so as not to wake the librarian up again. "When it comes to being on the ice, I really do know what I'm doing," she whispered.

As soon as Grace reached the courtyard, she could hear the excited voices of the other princesses drifting across the gardens from the lake.

This is it, she thought, pulling her hairy coat up around her ears and leaning down to strap a pair of home-made snowshoes to the bottom of her feet. They weren't real snowshoes like the ones she had at home, of course – just two old tennis rackets she had found behind an umbrella stand in the hall. But Fairy Godmother Webster had said she should dress up properly, and the flat racket heads would be just as good as the wooden snowshoes everyone in Cragland wore to cross the ice. She couldn't wait to see Precious's face when she slid on to the lake!

This will serve Precious right for all the times she has laughed at me for not knowing the right ballet steps, or how to hold a parasol, or which spoon to eat a pomegranate with, Grace thought. For once, she wouldn't be the worst princess in the class. When it came to ice, she was an expert – a real winter princess. After all, she came from Cragland – just about the coldest, snowiest, most frozen kingdom in the whole wide world. Better than that, she was a champion player at Fish Head Scoot, the wild slippery game Papa's warriors played using fishing holes in the frozen lakes. The idea was to score a goal by slipping an old fish head into the other team's ice hole. Meanwhile, you had to defend your own fishing pool with a big stick. Grace was a scooter, which meant it was her job to score as many goals as she could. She always tripped over her big flat feet when she tried to dance, but they were an advantage once she was out on the ice wearing enormous snowshoes.

"The bigger and flatter, the better, as Papa always says!" grinned Grace, hurtling round the side of a hedge and flinging herself at full speed on to the frozen lake.

"What are you wearing?" screamed Precious, laughing with delight as Grace scooted past her. "You look like a flat-footed yeti with those things on your feet."

"A flat-footed *hairy* yeti," snorted the twins, pointing at her enormous coat.

Precious circled round on a pair of bright white skates. The thin sharp blades flashed like diamonds in the pale winter sun.

"Oh!" Grace saw at once that she had made a mistake. All the other Tall Towers pupils wore little fur-trimmed skating dresses, just like Precious. They had thick fluffy mufflers to keep their hands warm and white ice skates which left delicate swirls like neat, curly handwriting on the frozen lake. Even the First Years were dressed the same.

"Of course!" Grace buried her head in her big hairy mittens and groaned. "The newest pupils in the school know more about being a princess than I do. I should have guessed skating at Tall Towers would be nothing like a game of Fish Head Scoot."

CHAPTER THREE
Skates

"Any good?" asked Scarlet.

Grace shook her head. She had abandoned her snowshoes outside the ballet studio at the side of the lake and was now trying to squeeze her feet into a tiny pair of proper-princess white skates.

Playtime was over and Fairy Godmother Flint was waiting for the Second Years out on the ice, ready to begin their first skating lesson.

"How about these?" Izumi dug to the

very back of the lost property cupboard and pulled out a big pair of ugly brown skates.

"I think they might have belonged to Sir Rolling-Trot," said Scarlet, squinting at the faded name scratched into the thick, worn leather.

"Probably," sighed Grace, thinking of the enormous riding coach with his long red beard. "He's just about the only person on the whole of Coronet Island who'd have skating boots big enough to fit me."

Sure enough, her feet slid comfortably into the wide brown skates. They weren't pretty, but they did fit.

"These will have to do," she said as Scarlet and Izumi helped her to her feet. "Whoa!" Grace's legs wobbled like a newborn giraffe as soon as she took her first step. "How do you even walk in these things?" she gasped, pointing down at the sharp blades as thin

as a knife. "I can barely stand up."

"It's easier once you're on the ice," said Scarlet kindly.

"Even though you've never worn skates before, you have winter royalty in your blood," encouraged Izumi, easing Grace towards the edge of the lake. "I bet you'll skate better than Glacia Blizzard, the famous ice star, once you get the hang of it."

"I wish I'd remembered Glacia Blizzard before I made an idiot of myself in my big flat snowshoes," groaned Grace. Even she had heard of the world-famous skater. She was known as "the ballerina of the ice".

Grace stared as her classmates spun and twirled and pirouetted across the frozen lake. "You couldn't do that in snowshoes!" she giggled. Even Flintheart looked elegant, gliding amongst the princesses like a swift black eagle.

"I wish I could skate as beautifully as Glacia Blizzard," said Scarlet with a sigh. "I'd love to be one of her Ice Maidens and dance in her shows."

"You probably could be," said Izumi. "Skating is just like dancing and you are the best in the class at that."

"Yikes!" squealed Grace, wobbling as her skates touched the ice. While Scarlet was the best dancer in the class, Grace was definitely the worst.

"Keep your head up!" said Scarlet. Grace's two friends held her hands and pulled her gently around the edge of the frozen lake.

"See?" said Izumi, after a while. "You're doing really well."

"Brilliant!" Scarlet agreed.

"Do you think so?" Grace grinned. She did feel she might be getting the hang of it. Her long legs weren't wobbling quite as much as they had been at the start. They'd been skating for nearly five minutes already and she hadn't fallen over once – that would be a record if she was learning a tricky new step in ballet class.

"Go on then," she said. "Let me try on my own."

"If you're sure..." said Izumi. Her friends let go.

"Head up!" said Scarlet.

"Shoulders back!" cried Izumi.

"Whoops!" Grace stumbled forward. She took three shaky, slippery, sliding steps – waving her arms like a windmill – but did not fall over.

"Phew!" she grinned. "That was a close one!" No sooner had Grace spoken than her skates slipped from underneath her and she landed flat on her bottom.

"Ha!" Precious swooshed by with her nose in the air. "What are you doing down there? Playing Fish Head Splat?" she laughed.

"The game is called Fish Head *Scoot*," scowled Grace.

Flintheart swept across the ice. Her sharp black skates skidded to a stop and she peered down her long thin nose at Grace. "Perhaps you would like a chair?" she asked.

"Er..." Grace was flabbergasted. It was unlike the strict teacher to be so kind. But she realized she'd love to sit down, just for a moment. Her laces were coming undone and the clumpy brown skates weighed a ton. "A chair would be wonderful," she said with a grateful smile.

"Very well." The fairy godmother motioned to a Tall Towers groom who was standing at the edge of the lake. He slid on to the ice, carrying one of the small gold chairs the princesses usually sat on to watch dance recitals and shows.

"Thank you so much," said Grace, flopping gratefully on to the little gold seat.

"Whatever are you doing?" cried Fairy Godmother Flint.

"Er ... sitting down," said Grace, but she leapt instantly back to her wobbly feet.

"I didn't fetch a chair for you to sit on," sighed Flintheart. "I fetched it so that you wouldn't fall over. Here." She took Grace's hands and placed them firmly on the back of the chair. "Hold tight. Push it in front of you like a trolley. I'm sure you used something similar when you first learned to walk."

Grace blushed. The fairy godmother was right. Tucked away in the nursery at home there was an old push-along yak on wooden wheels. Grace and Pip had both loved the toy when they first learned to toddle about. But even Pip had grown out of it years ago.

"What a baby!" snorted Precious, holding one leg out behind her in a corkscrew spin. "Imagine having to skate with a chair."

"Go stuff a snowball up your nose," snapped Grace, sticking her tongue out at her cousin. She didn't care how babyish *that* made her look. "Blurrr!"

"Proper princesses do not stick out their tongues," said Fairy Godmother Flint. "If anybody else needs a chair, please join Grace and keep to the edge of the ice. Otherwise, follow me to the centre of the lake. We are going to work on our ankle holds and spins."

"See you later." Grace waved to Scarlet and Izumi as the whole class glided off across the ice like a flock of elegant swans, their white skating dresses rustling in the chilly breeze.

I'm more like a penguin than a swan, Grace thought, waddling away behind her chair.

To make things worse, Lady DuLac, the beautiful Tall Towers headmistress, was skating towards her now. She looked like a snow queen in her long blue cloak and matching skates.

"Excuse me, Fairy Godmother," the headmistress called. "I am sorry to interrupt your class, but I have an announcement to make."

Grace felt a tingle of excitement. The headmistress was smiling, so it was obviously good news.

"Glacia Blizzard, the famous ice dancer, is coming to Tall Towers," said Lady DuLac. "She is going to perform a brand-new show here on the lake."

"Glacia Blizzard? Coming here?" The princesses swarmed around the headmistress, skidding, spinning, screaming and hugging each other with delight. "When's she coming? How long will she stay? Will we all be able to see the show?"

Usually it was clumsy Grace who crashed

into people or tripped them over, but now *she* was the one being buffeted about like a leaf in a snowstorm by the crowd of excited princesses. She gripped tightly to her chair. "Whoa!" she cried as Scarlet and Izumi spun her in a circle.

"Young Majesties!" cried Flintheart. "This is a most un-princess-like way to behave!"

Nobody paid the slightest attention. "Glacia Blizzard is coming!" they cheered. "She is going to skate on the Tall Towers lake!"

CHAPTER FOUR
The Queen of Winter

The following afternoon, every princess in the school was gathered on the quayside, hoping to catch the first glimpse of Glacia Blizzard's ship as it came into view.

"We'll never see anything from back here," sighed Scarlet, pointing at the rows of older girls who had taken the best spots along the harbour wall.

"At least you're tall," said tiny Izumi, looking up at Grace. "All I can see is the back of people's heads. I wish I could sit on your shoulders."

"I've got a better plan," laughed Grace. "Follow me."

The three friends hurried up the steep coastal path that led along the edge of the cliffs.

"This was the perfect spot for dragon-watching last year," said Grace, scrambling up into the icy branches of a small tree. "I'm sure it will be good for spotting famous ice dancers too."

"Brilliant idea," said Scarlet and Izumi as they swung up beside her.

"I brought these as well." Grace pulled a pair of old binoculars out of her coat pocket and peered through them. "Look! There's a ship!" she cried. Sure enough, a tall white sailing vessel came slowly into view.

"That must be Glacia Blizzard," said Izumi as the ship turned towards Coronet Island.

"I can't believe she's going to perform a brand-new show just for us," quivered Scarlet. "It's about the most thrilling thing ever to happen at Tall Towers."

The ship slid silently through the silvery water as Grace peered down through the frosted branches. It was far more beautiful than she could ever have expected. The sails were as white and feathery as frost on a window, and the three great masts rose up like sharpened icicles towards the snowy sky. Even the hull looked as if it was made of frosted glass or carved from ice. "Brrr." Looking at it made Grace shiver with cold – as if it had floated right from the heart of a frozen world.

"The *Queen of Winter*," she mouthed, reading the name of the ship, which was written in pale letters on the prow.

"But there's nobody out on the deck,"

sighed Scarlet, leaning forward as the vessel came closer to the shore. "The skaters must all be keeping warm below."

"Wait!" Grace squinted through the binoculars. "There is somebody. But I don't think she's a skater."

A little old lady had stepped out from behind one of the icy sails. She stared up at the sky, paying no attention to the clamouring crowd of princesses waiting on the dock.

The Queen of Winter

"Well, that's not Glacia Blizzard," whispered Grace. She knew that the famous dancer was elegant, young and beautiful. This woman's back was bent double with age and her hair was white as snow.

The old lady lifted her head quite suddenly and peered at the cliff above. It was as if she knew the three friends were up there.

Grace shuddered.

"What's the matter?" asked Scarlet.

"Nothing," Grace fibbed. "It's just the cold." But something about the old lady's icy stare had sent a shiver down her spine. "That's odd. The geese are coming back," she said, pointing to a V of birds, flying into view. "It's as if they are following the ship."

The old lady had seen them too. She lifted her head and stared. Through the binoculars, Grace was sure she saw her smile.

"Something's not right," she said, scratching

her head. "I saw the geese flying south when I was in the library yesterday. Geese never turn back once they've left for the winter."

The white birds flew straight towards the sailing ship, as if they were being pulled by an invisible string.

The old woman stood as still as a block of ice and watched them sweep across the darkening sky towards her.

CHAPTER FIVE
Fire and Ice

As soon as the geese reached the ship, a thick white mist rolled in, so Grace didn't see where they went.

The *Queen of Winter* dropped her sails and stayed resting out at sea.

"Why doesn't Glacia's ship come into harbour?" asked Scarlet.

"Perhaps she's waiting for the mist to clear," said Izumi as they scrambled down the path to join the other princesses. They found the Second Years bunched together, leaning over a low corner of the harbour wall. The misty grey sky had turned black. A velvet, wintry darkness fell over Coronet Island.

"I think that's it for the night," said Grace, stamping her feet and blowing on her fingers.

But the *Queen of Winter* suddenly burst into light.

Boom!

Everyone cheered as the night sky above the ship was filled with fireworks, shooting into the air like molten diamonds.

"Look!" said Izumi. "They've made the shape of a pair of silver skates."

"Wow!" Grace leant so far back she almost toppled over. The fireworks were beautiful, making a pattern like a hundred falling snowflakes as the white ship moved forward towards the harbour. If this display was just for Glacia Blizzard's arrival on Coronet

The Queen of Winter

Island, the skating show was going to be something really special.

Once the ship had docked, a great frozen gangplank was lowered. Two dancers, in skating tutus made of silvery white feathers, glided silently on to the icy surface. Each held a flaming torch. As they slid forward with the fire crackling in their hands, another pair of skaters appeared, then another, until there were twelve dancers altogether, each holding a burning torch. The icy gangplank blazed with light.

The beautiful young women fluttered their arms and stretched, twirling slowly on one leg as if they had been woken from a frozen dream. They descended, leaving the glistening gangplank and gliding down to the mouth of the icy river that led from the harbour to the lake. The wintry world of Coronet Island turned orange from their glowing flames.

"Which one is Glacia Blizzard, do you think?" hissed Grace, tugging at Scarlet's sleeve.

"Don't be ridiculous!" said Precious, barging between the friends to get a better view. "Those are just the skating Ice Maidens. Glacia herself hasn't come off the ship."

"Look out!" Precious pushed her roughly aside, and Grace was jostled to the back of the crowd. She lost sight of the gangplank for a moment, but she could tell that something exciting was happening. The cheers and shouts which had rung out all evening suddenly ceased. There was a frozen hush, then a gasp from everybody on the quay.

"What is it?" Grace stood up on tiptoes . . . and then she gasped too.

Glacia Blizzard stepped lightly off the end of the gangplank. She was tall – the tallest woman Grace had ever seen – but not gangly like Grace, whose legs were long and skinny (like strands of spaghetti, she always thought). Glacia looked strong and sleek. She had icy blonde hair and skin as pale as snow, like a white marble statue of a goddess or a warrior. Glacia Blizzard truly was the most beautiful woman Grace had ever seen.

"Gosh!" Grace squeezed in beside Izumi and pointed to a spiky, shimmering crown of icicles on Glacia's head. "She really is the Queen of Winter, just like the name of her ship."

The famous dancer did not have a burning torch, but she shone more brightly than any of the Ice Maidens. Dazzling silvery gems twinkled like icicles on her dress.

"I bet they're diamonds," gasped Precious. "That's so unfair. I want a diamond dress."

"So do we!" whined the twins.

The torchlit procession parted and Glacia Blizzard spun all the way to the front on the tip of one skate.

"What a wonderful move!" cried Scarlet.

The crowd of princesses ran along the edge of the riverbank.

"She's so fast," gasped Grace. She was amazed how long and elegant Glacia's stride was. Three pushes forward on her skates and she was already at the bend in the river by the gardens.

The princesses followed, cheering louder than ever.

As the fiery parade reached the mouth of the lake, Glacia Blizzard came to a stop. She raised her arms and spoke to the crowd. "Worthy headmistress, kind fairy godmothers and elegant young princesses," she began in a clear, rich voice, "it is a great honour to come to Coronet Island and visit your famous school – the finest princess academy in all the world." A cheer of pride filled the cold night air. "I long to skate on your lake and to share my new show with you. It is called 'The Frozen Heart'. I shall perform it for you on Saturday night as soon as the sky is dark."

"At night?" said Grace. "How exciting!"

Scarlet was right – this was just about the most thrilling thing ever to happen at Tall Towers school.

But now the white mist was rolling back in from the sea, wrapping itself around Glacia Blizzard like a cloak. The Ice Maidens raised their burning lights in the air, which suddenly flickered and went out, as if a single blast of icy wind had caught them. As the fiery glow faded, the performers vanished too, melting into the frozen mist.

Grace held her breath, desperate to see them again. She leant forward, longing to catch another glimpse of Glacia Blizzard. But, when the icy cloud cleared, the famous skater and her dancers had disappeared. It was as if they had become part of the icy lake itself.

CHAPTER SIX
The Ice Pavilion

The three friends woke early next morning.

"I was too excited about Glacia Blizzard to sleep a wink," said Scarlet.

"Me too," agreed Izumi.

"Let's go down to the lake," said Grace, leaping up from the floor after having fallen out of bed as usual. "Perhaps Glacia and the Ice Maidens will be rehearsing their show."

It had snowed again all through the night, and the friends left three sets of fresh footprints as they hurried across the gardens.

"Look." Grace stopped and pointed down the hill towards the frozen lake. "What's that?"

On the far shore, a magnificent building had sprung up overnight. It was round and gleaming, as large as a church and very grand. A big bright dome rose in the middle with two smaller ones on either side.

"It's a pavilion," said Izumi. "Like a winter palace of some sort."

"Is it made of glass?" asked Scarlet as the girls crept around the lake.

"Not glass," said Izumi. "Ice."

"You're right," whispered Grace once they were close enough that she could stretch out her hand and touch the cold, carved walls of the pavilion. Even the simple igloos Papa's warriors built could take half a day to make. "This must have taken hours. It's as if magic snow fairies have come in the night and built it," she laughed.

Scarlet and Izumi shook their heads in wonder.

Facing the lake was an arched doorway. Like everything else, the polished doorknob was made of ice, and it was carved like a frosted heart.

"This must be where Glacia Blizzard and the Ice Maidens are staying," said Grace. She couldn't resist. She tiptoed forward and turned the handle.

"Don't touch it!" Scarlet, who was always nervous, almost ran away. But nothing happened. The big cold door wouldn't open.

"It's frozen shut," whispered Grace. She pressed her face against the frosted building and tried to peer inside. Even though the walls were made of ice, they were far too thick to see through.

"We shouldn't be here," said Scarlet. "Let's go."

But it was too late. The door swung open with a sound of cracking ice.

"Can I help?" The voice was like ice too – cold and crackling with frost.

"Er, no... Sorry." Grace shivered as she stared at the hunched figure in the doorway. It was the little old woman they had seen on the ship.

Grace's heart was pounding. It was all she could do not to turn and flee. The old lady's skin was dull and grey like thick puddle-water ice. Her head was stooped and her thin fingers were bent like frosty twigs on a winter tree.

"My name is Miss Wintermore," she said. "I am Glacia Blizzard's wardrobe mistress. I

look after the costumes for the show and, of course, the skates."

"Oh!" Grace breathed a sigh of relief as the wardrobe mistress stepped out into the dawn light. She was just an ordinary, hard-working old lady. "Nice to meet you." Grace blushed with shame to think how harshly she had judged her for the way she looked. It was the sort of thing Precious would do.

"I am sorry if we woke you," she said with a little wobbly curtsy. Izumi and Scarlet curtsied too.

Miss Wintermore's face softened. "You have the elegance of a dancer," she said, smiling at Scarlet. "I expect you are very good on the ice."

"Oh, not really," said Scarlet. "I haven't had much practice. I come from a warm kingdom, you see. And when I go too fast, I get a little afraid."

"Don't listen to her – she's brilliant," said Grace.

"Fear is something you must conquer," the old lady said. "I know Miss Blizzard would agree." Next she looked Izumi up and down. "You have a sense of style, my dear. I can tell from the way you wear your clothes."

Now it was Izumi's turn to blush.

"She is an amazing artist and she designs her own outfits for different dances and things," said Grace, knowing Izumi would never say so herself.

"Ah." Miss Wintermore smiled softly and her old face lit up. "I expect you'd like to see the costumes for the show."

"Oh, yes," Izumi beamed. "I'd love that. I can't imagine how you made the ice dress Glacia Blizzard wore last night."

"I'm afraid I'm very busy right now, but you can come back this afternoon if you ask your teacher's permission," said the wardrobe mistress kindly.

"Thank you." Izumi grinned as if she had just unwrapped the most exciting birthday present in the world.

"Bring your friends too," said Miss Wintermore as Grace stood on tiptoes and tried to peer over her shoulder into the icy hallway beyond. "And what is your special talent, I wonder?" she asked. She looked at Grace's hairy yak coat. "You do not worry about what you wear, I see. And you are no dancer either."

"No." Grace came down from her wobbly tiptoes. "It's true." It was at times like this she wished she were more of a proper princess. All the other royal girls seemed to have particular gifts to help them be more elegant and graceful, like a true princess should be.

"But I see you have great curiosity," said Miss Wintermore. "And I suspect you have courage too."

"She does!" said Scarlet.

Grace smiled weakly. She might be brave – and a little nosy – but sometimes she'd also like to be able to do a perfect pirouette.

"Come back later and you may look around. But you won't catch a glimpse of Miss Blizzard," said the old lady firmly. "Not until nightfall."

She shuffled inside and closed the magnificent door with a slow, cold creak.

CHAPTER SEVEN
Costumes

Flintheart grudgingly gave permission for the girls to return to the ice pavilion and see the costumes later that day.

"As long as you don't become a nuisance," she sniffed, staring particularly hard at Grace. "Keep your sticky fingers to yourselves and mind where you put your feet."

"Yes, Fairy Godmother," promised Grace. Then, before she left, she dashed down to the stables to take Billy a bucket of warm pomegranate juice in case he was feeling chilly.

"I wouldn't have missed this for the world," she whispered as she caught up with Scarlet and Izumi. Miss Wintermore opened the door to the pavilion and they stepped in to the high domed hallway. Everything was made entirely of ice. Grace glimpsed a frozen spiral staircase, twisting to the floor as if a cascading waterfall had been enchanted while it flowed.

"This way to the wardrobe," said Miss Wintermore, leading them down a slippery corridor to a room full of frosted coat pegs.

"Oh my goodness!" said Izumi.

The costumes were amazing. Row upon row of ice-blue, snow-white and misty-silver outfits hung from frozen rails.

"Come." Miss Wintermore beckoned Izumi over to examine a floor-length frosted gown. Grace recognized it as the one Glacia Blizzard had worn last night.

"Are these diamonds?" asked Izumi, pointing to the jagged shimmering jewels which covered every centimetre of the frock.

"No. Not diamonds," laughed Miss Wintermore. "Feel them."

The girls stretched out their hands.

"Icicles," said Grace as a cold pain shot through her.

"That's right." Miss Wintermore nodded and moved the dress away from their clasping fingers. "Careful. If this gown gets too warm, it will melt away to nothing but a pool of water."

Grace saw that many of the grandest outfits were not weaved from cloth at all, but were twisted, frozen sculptures made of ice. These were Glacia Blizzard's costumes. Only the Ice Maidens wore sequins and silk.

"If you like, you can help with some of these," said Miss Wintermore, piling twelve blue satin leotards into Izumi's outstretched arms. "I alone work on Miss Blizzard's costumes, but the Ice Maidens need sequins and feathers sewn all along the collars and cuffs."

"I'd love to help," said Izumi with a grin of pride. To Grace, who hated sewing, it seemed like an awful lot of work. But she knew if Sir Rolling-Trot asked her to groom every unicorn in the stable she would leap at the chance without worrying for one moment how long it would take.

Izumi squeezed her arm. "I'm so excited," she whispered. And Grace felt she almost understood.

"Carry them back to school and work on them there," said Miss Wintermore. "Just so long as they are ready in time for the show on Saturday night."

"They will be," Izumi promised.

"It is getting late now," said Miss

Wintermore. Grace was amazed how long they had spent amongst the costumes. It had grown dim and gloomy inside the ice pavilion. As it was winter, and they had come so late in the afternoon, it must already be nearly dark outside.

"Quickly," said Miss Wintermore, suddenly flustered. "Show yourselves out. I have to see Miss Blizzard now." She shuffled hurriedly away, disappearing through a narrow door hidden between two rails of costumes. The door shut firmly behind her.

"How odd," whispered Grace. "Why was she in such a hurry?"

"I suppose she must be very busy," said Scarlet.

"Let's go." Izumi started back towards the door. "We were lucky Miss Wintermore let us visit at all."

Grace knew her friend was right, but she

was itching to peek into the other rooms –
and maybe even catch a glimpse of Glacia
Blizzard. Surely she would be up now after
her long rest?

"Come on!" said Izumi.

Grace slipped and slithered across the
great domed hallway to catch up with her
friends. She slid to a wobbly stop in front
of Izumi, whose arms were full of costumes,
and opened the heavy ice door.

"It's sunset," Grace gasped. A dark red
winter sun was just dipping down on the
horizon, as if sinking into the sea.

"How beautiful," said Izumi.

Grace raised her hand to her eyes and
squinted at the crimson sky. "Look. It's the
geese again!" she said. This time they were
flying towards the ice pavilion.

"They still haven't left the island then?"
said Scarlet.

"I don't understand it," said Grace. She turned to shut the door and jumped with surprise.

Glacia Blizzard herself was standing at the top of the frozen spiral staircase watching the three friends leave.

CHAPTER EIGHT
Skating Practice

From the first moment she saw Glacia Blizzard, Grace was determined to get better at skating. Now, when she wasn't taking warm treats to Billy in the stables, she spent all her free time on the lake. There was a rumour the famous ice star might come and watch the princesses skate. If that was true, Grace was desperate to make a good impression – or, at least, to try not to fall flat on her face.

Every lesson, she pushed her little gold

chair round and round the edge of the lake, her back getting straighter and her legs less wobbly each time.

Precious and the twins seemed to have nothing better to do than to wait for her to finish a lap and roar with laughter as she passed by.

"Sit down before you fall down!" giggled Precious. She had demanded to be sent new skating gear from home and was now wearing a feather tutu like the Ice Maidens and a sparkly top which said FUTURE ICE STAR in sequins across the front. She also had brand-new skates with P.P. written in glitter on the toes.

"You probably think it stands for Princess Precious," she said, pirouetting past Grace and laughing at her brown borrowed skates for the hundredth time. "But Daddy says P.P. can stand for Perfect Princess too."

"Or Posh Pest!" muttered Grace under her breath. She wished Precious would leave her alone.

Scarlet and Izumi waved whenever they swooshed by. They had teamed up with Princess Rosamond and Princess Juliette and were practising a complicated ice dance routine. Princess Latisha and Princess Martine joined in and the six Second Year girls spun around each other, sweeping in and out in an elegant snowflake pattern and spinning close to the ice on one leg.

Grace would have given anything to be able to join them, but she knew that if she did, she would be bruised black and blue from falling over. Worse than that, she would spoil the whole routine.

"I'm safer leaning on my chair," she told herself. After years of flat snowshoes, she still felt as if she was trying to walk on the wobbly blades of a pair of scissors.

Right leg forward, left leg forward, right leg forward, left leg forward... she repeated in her head. Then, at last, she let go of the chair and skated slowly all the way around the lake – without tripping over.

"I did it!" she cried.

The whole class cheered – all except Precious and the twins. Even Flintheart smiled. "Very good!" she said. "You can leave your chair behind tomorrow."

As dusk fell, Flintheart blew her whistle to signal the end of class and beckoned to the girls to join her in the middle of the lake.

"Look," said Grace, grabbing Izumi's arm as they skated together towards their teacher.

From the other end of the lake, where the ice pavilion was, the flames of twelve flickering torches shimmered on the ice.

As the lights came closer, Grace saw that the torches were being carried by the Ice Maidens. At the centre of the group, like a shining silver planet surrounded by fiery moons, was Glacia Blizzard.

"Isn't she magnificent!" whispered Grace, seeing again how tall and strong the skater was. "What do you suppose she wants?"

Before anyone could answer, the ice star called out to them. "Young Majesties, Fairy Godmother ... could I keep you here for just one moment? I have a favour to ask."

"Of course," Flintheart answered. The princesses leant forward on their skates. What sort of favour could Glacia Blizzard possibly want from them?

"I need somebody to skate in my show," the ice star said simply.

"I'll do it!" Precious barged forward.

"Or me," said Scarlet softly.

Or me, thought Grace – though she knew it was hopeless to dream she'd ever be picked, so she didn't dare to say it out loud.

"When do I start?" said Precious, swishing across the ice and practically grabbing Glacia by the arm. "What do I have to do?"

"One moment," said Fairy Godmother Flint. "If Miss Blizzard is looking for a Second Year to skate in her show, then I will pick the pupil who will take part."

"Oh, good. If Flintheart's choosing, she'll be bound to pick you," whispered Grace, squeezing Scarlet's arm. All hopes of her own had quickly turned to pride for her friend. "You're the best skater in the class by far, even though Precious has been learning for twice as long."

But Glacia Blizzard raised her hand. "Pardon me, Fairy Godmother," she said firmly. "As it is my show, I will choose the princess who will skate."

"Gosh!" whispered Grace, a mixture of excitement and shock fizzing in her tummy.

She had never heard anybody contradict Flintheart before.

"As you wish," the teacher sniffed.

"Auditions will be held at dusk on Wednesday night," said Glacia. "That's just two days from now. Each of you has a chance to prove your skill at the audition … but I will only choose one skater from amongst you all."

CHAPTER NINE
The Sneeze

During every spare moment they had, the Second Years could be found on the ice.

Glacia Blizzard had told them they must audition with a short solo they had choreographed themselves.

"Pretend you are a young frost fairy exploring the winter world," she explained. "The princess who is picked will be the one whose audition moves me most – the girl who skates with all her heart and soul."

Nearly every Second Year was going to try

for the role. Only Izumi decided she was too busy with the costumes to take part. Grace didn't really see herself as a dainty frost fairy, but there was nothing to lose. She would make up a short dance for the audition and give it her best shot — heart and soul!

"Whee!" she cried, skidding across the lake as she practised gliding from side to side. She couldn't skate backwards yet or twist and turn in tight circles but, as long as she was going forwards with both feet on the ground, she could move quite fast. She pretended she was playing Fish Head Scoot, dodging like a whirlwind between the other skaters to score a goal.

"My poor little fairy is being tossed about in a storm," she explained to Scarlet as she whooshed and swooshed across the ice, clapping her hands and roaring to sound like thunder.

"That's brilliant," squealed Scarlet, her hair flying up as Grace whooshed past. "I really do feel as if I'm in a storm."

"Let's have a look at your dance," panted Grace, staggering to the side of the lake and collapsing on to a bench. "I think I overdid the thunder a bit."

"It's not very good yet," said the red-haired princess, shyly. "I'm trying to show how the young fairy learns to fly on a snowy morning."

"Go on!" urged Grace, bending to retie her laces, which had come undone yet again.

At first, she was only half watching as she fiddled with her boots. But Grace soon forgot all about her laces and stared at Scarlet with her mouth wide open. Even though it was only a rough rehearsal and all the other princesses were out on the ice, she couldn't take her eyes off her friend. The shy princess so perfectly became a delicate, inquisitive fairy, exploring the power of her new wings. Grace laughed out loud as Scarlet showed the little sprite imitating the falling snowflakes, her frosty fingers stretched out wide. The best bit of all was when the fairy finally left the ground. Scarlet leapt

into the air, her arms spread like wings as she turned ... three ... four ... *five* times above the ice. Then she spun away, leaping, twisting and spiralling with the joy of flight, until she sunk down and ended the dance in the splits.

"Whoopee!" Grace leapt to her feet, wobbling on her skates and cheering with delight. "That was amazing!" Out of the corner of her eye, she saw Precious scowling with fury. Most of the other princesses were watching too. There was no doubt about it, Scarlet would steal the show.

With the auditions so close, the Second Years would have stayed out on the ice all day if they could. They were desperate to spend every last minute perfecting their solos, putting finishing touches to each twist and turn.

"Not this lunchtime," said Fairy Godmother McKenzie, the sporty Sixth-Form teacher, striding into the dining room where the princesses were just finishing their pudding. "My class are going to be on the lake practising a complicated figure-skating routine. It is closed to other students, I am afraid."

"That is so unfair!" raged Precious, banging her fists on the dining-room table.

Grace was a little relieved. She had angry red blisters on her toes from the borrowed skating boots, and her knees and bottom were bruised from where she still kept falling down.

"It will do us all good to have a break," she said, seeing how Scarlet was biting her lip, clearly worried about her routine. "You too!" She wagged her finger at Izumi. "You were up half the night making those costumes. It's time you had some fun."

"Yes, miss," Izumi laughed. Scarlet giggled too. They weren't used to Grace being the sensible one.

"Come on!" Grace leapt up. The idea she'd just had was nothing to do with being sensible at all. "I'll show you how to have some proper winter fun ... Cragland style!" She seized a big silver serving tray from the table and they hurried towards the door. "This will make a brilliant sledge."

The Tall Towers trays were big enough to serve tea to at least twelve princesses at a time, so there was plenty of room for the three friends to squeeze on board. Grace sat at the back, Scarlet in the middle and Izumi, who was smallest, perched on the front.

"Ready?" asked Grace as they teetered at the top of the big meadow that sloped down towards the stables.

"Ready!" cheered Izumi. Scarlet made

a small, frightened gulping sound, which Grace guessed meant "yes".

"Here goes!" she said, leaning back and pushing off with her hands.

"WHEE!" The tea tray shot forward like a bullet. It made a perfect sledge, slipping and slithering down the snowy hill at top speed.

Grace's plaits blew out behind her. "Whoopee!" she cheered.

The tray bounced over a frozen tussock of grass and flew through the air like a magic carpet. As it hit the snow again it spun around so that the girls whizzed down the rest of the hill facing backwards. They landed in a giggling heap beside a frozen haystack.

Scarlet was first to jump to her feet. "Again!" she cried. Grace and Izumi laughed. Scarlet was so often afraid to try new things but was as brave as anyone once she'd had a

go. "I can't believe I've never been sledging before," she said.

"Me neither," agreed Izumi.

Again and again the girls sped down the hill and tumbled into the snow at the bottom. Once, they ended up head first in the snowy haystack, six legs sticking out like teaspoons in a bowl of white sugar.

"We look like snowmen," laughed Scarlet, staggering to her feet.

"Snow princesses, actually," said Grace with a wobbly curtsy.

"Good job Flintheart can't see us," grinned Izumi as they brushed themselves down.

"*A proper princess does not sledge on a tea tray*," Grace mimicked, peering down her nose at her friends.

At last, lunch break was over. Soaking wet and exhausted from the snow, the laughing girls hurried back to change into dry clothes before afternoon classes.

"The trouble with proper princesses," smiled Grace, dragging the tea tray behind her, "is that sometimes, they don't know how to have fun."

"True," said Izumi, shaking snow from her collar.

Scarlet nodded and let out a little sneeze. "Achoo!"

"Oh no! I hope you're not getting a chill," said Grace. "Not before the audition tomorrow night."

Perhaps sledging really wasn't the most sensible idea, after all, she thought.

CHAPTER TEN
The Auditions

Next morning, Scarlet's nose was red, her eyes were puffy and she had lost her voice.

"Off to the sickbay with you, Young Majesty," said kind Fairy Godmother Pom, as she spotted Scarlet struggling down the stairs with her skates in her hand.

"I..." Scarlet shook her head and tried desperately to speak.

"No arguments!" said Fairy Godmother Pom. The jolly seamstress was as strict as a mother bear when it came to sickness.

"You need a warm bed and plenty of rest."

"But we need to practise – our auditions for Glacia Blizzard's show are tonight," Grace explained. "Scarlet is sure to get the part. I know she will."

"Not if she's sick in bed," sneered Precious with a nasty little laugh. She pushed past them on the stairs, her specially initialled skates clanking noisily in her hand.

"*Please*," begged Grace, throwing herself in front of the fairy godmother. "Scarlet *has* to go to that audition." The thought of the smug smile on Precious's face if she got the part was more than Grace could bear. "If only we hadn't gone sledging," she groaned.

"You don't know that's what made Scarlet ill," said Fairy Godmother Pom. "A chill like this could have been coming on for days. I'm not surprised with the hours you've all spent on the ice." She put her arm round

Scarlet's shoulders. "If you want any chance of going to that audition tonight, the best thing you can do is go to bed and get a good rest. With a bit of luck, you might feel better by this evening."

But, as the day went on, Scarlet's temperature rose higher and higher. The doctor was called after lunch.

"Scarlet has a fever," he said. "She must stay in bed for at least twenty-four hours."

"So that's it," sighed Grace as the grey, wintry afternoon slipped into darkness. "She'll never make it to the audition now."

"I'm afraid not," agreed Izumi as they trudged across the snowy gardens towards the lake. All the excitement of performing for Glacia Blizzard had disappeared like a melting snowflake.

"It's so unfair," raged Grace. "Scarlet's dance was perfect. She would definitely have got the role."

"If only the auditions could be postponed," said Izumi. "Scarlet might be well enough tomorrow."

But, as they turned the corner, they saw that the lake was ablaze with torches. Strings of pretty white fairy lights were strung above the ice. Everything was all set to take place tonight.

"No Scarlet, then?" said Precious. Her smile glinted in the torchlight. She was wearing her special P.P. skates, ready to show off her dance (something about a frost fairy looking at herself in the mirror). From the way she was grinning, you'd think she had already got the part.

"Why is Glacia Blizzard holding the auditions after dark?" said Grace crossly. Even the glow of the torches and twinkling lights couldn't cheer her up. For the first time all winter, she felt properly cold. "Surely this would be easier in the daylight?"

"The ice is always being used for lessons and things," said Izumi. "Perhaps the teachers don't want their timetables disrupted too much."

"Maybe." Grace shrugged, remembering how Fairy Godmother McKenzie had closed the rink for her Sixth Formers. "It's funny though. Have you noticed we've only ever seen Glacia and her Ice Maidens after dark?"

"Honestly," Precious butted in, "you don't know anything about being a star, do you, Grace? It's all part of the drama … the *mystery*." She pointed to the flickering lights. "Not that I'd expect you to understand; you're from Cragland." She laughed nastily. "Your idea of a good show is watching a seal juggle fish!"

"A seal," honked the twins. "Hilarious!"

"I don't know about seals, but there was a juggling walrus once," said Grace quite seriously. "He was amazing. He could spin seven mackerel in one go."

"You see!" Precious and the twins collapsed in laughter.

"What's so funny?" asked Grace.

Izumi led her away. "Time to put your skates on," she said. "You have an audition to do. We need to make Scarlet proud."

Just then a hush fell over the ice. A tall, proud figure had appeared on the far side of the lake.

"It's Glacia Blizzard," whispered Visalotta, joining Izumi and Grace.

The Second Years peered forwards excitedly as the famous ice dancer slid down the frozen slope from the pavilion. She was alone this time with no Ice Maidens beside her.

Glacier Blizzard skated to the centre of the rink and raised her slender arms like a swaying silver birch tree.

"Welcome, Young Majesties. Dazzle me with your auditions," she cried. Then she sat gently down on the same little gold chair that Grace had pushed around the ice. "Let the contest begin."

"You first, Truffle," said Precious, pushing the startled twin on to the ice. She looked round at the other Second Years. "I'm going last. I want to make a big impression."

Poor Truffle was totally thrown. She stumbled round the ice, forgetting all her moves.

Trinket followed, and didn't fare much better.

Sports-mad Princess Latisha went next and did a wonderful, leaping dance which Grace admired for its speed and agility.

"Whoops!" Grace gasped as Latisha took the last corner a little too quickly and almost overbalanced. She righted herself just in time, but her face was frozen in horror with the fear of falling over in front of a crowd. Grace knew that feeling all too well.

Visalotta's dance was lovely, and the diamonds on her skating boots glinted like enchanted icicles beneath the fairy lights. Theatrical Princess Juliette brought the cheeky character of her fairy to life brilliantly. And Princess Martine, who had a wonderful singing voice, ended her dance with a winter song. All of the auditions were strong but none was as perfect as Scarlet's would have been.

"Go on!" said Precious, pushing Grace towards the ice. "Get your disaster over and done with, then I'll show Glacia Blizzard what a proper princess can do."

"Watch out!" cried Grace. Her lace had come undone yet again and Precious was standing on it with her sharp skates. *Ping!* The lace snapped.

"Oh no," sighed Grace. The frayed end was far too short to tie into a knot.

"I've got a piece of string somewhere," said Izumi. "We can mend it."

"You'll have to go before me, Precious," said Grace as Glacia Blizzard waved for the next audition to start.

"Typical!" Precious scowled. But Glacia waved again and the spoilt princess had no choice but to head out on to the ice and begin her audition whether she liked it or not.

Grace bent down and fumbled with the string, trying to tie it to the stubby end of her broken lace.

"Here. Let me," said Izumi. "You're all fingers and thumbs."

It was only as Grace looked up that she saw what Precious was doing out on the lake.

"Stop!" she cried. "You can't do that. That's Scarlet's dance."

CHAPTER ELEVEN
Scarlet's Dance

Precious had stolen every move of Scarlet's carefully choreographed routine. Grace watched in horror, gripping Izumi's hand, as Precious pretended to explore the power of her new-found wings, then imitated the falling snowflakes, her fingers stretched out wide.

Although Precious would never have had the imagination to come up with the dance for herself, she had enough skill to do the steps well. Two, three, four turns; not quite the five that Scarlet had managed – and not landing quite as lightly either, or leaping with such grace – but good enough to be the best audition of the evening ... by *far*.

As she finished the dance, flinging herself into the splits – though not half as low as Scarlet – Precious grinned with satisfaction. Glacia Blizzard rose to her feet and clapped. It was her first standing ovation of the night.

"That's it," said Visalotta. "Precious has the part for sure."

"But don't you see?" said Grace. "She used Scarlet's dance to get it. It's not fair. I have to tell Glacia Blizzard what Precious has done."

"Not yet," said Izumi as Glacia called for the next audition. "Do your piece first, or she might think you're complaining just so you can get the part yourself."

"Izumi's right," agreed Visalotta. "We

ought to wait until everybody has danced."

"Fine." Grace wiggled her feet to check that the string on her laces would hold.

"Top that!" whooped Precious, skating triumphantly off the ice, her fists raised in victory.

If Grace was supposed to be skating like a fairy caught in a winter storm, she certainly had a hurricane raging inside her.

Whoosh! She flew across the ice, faster than she had ever skated before.

Swoosh! How dare Precious steal Scarlet's moves?

Whoosh! She wasn't going to get away with it.

Swoosh! Scarlet would have danced twice as well as Precious.

Wh ... wh ... whoa! Grace was skating so furiously she skidded right off the far end of the lake.

"Ouch!" She landed in a spiky patch of frozen reeds. The string on her broken bootlace snapped again, her leg shot up in the air and her heavy brown skate spun around – three, four, *five* times – and landed in a tree.

Grace staggered to her feet, wobbling on one skate.

Visalotta and Izumi were speeding across the ice towards her. "Are you all right?" they cried. "Are you hurt?"

"I'm fine," said Grace. But it was over. Glacia Blizzard's little gold chair was empty. She had gone.

The Ice Maidens swept silently from the pavilion. Lifting Precious on to their shoulders, they carried her around the rink in a lap of honour.

"P.P. for Prize Performer," cheered Precious, clicking the heels of her skates and pointing to the sequin letters on her toes.

"Perfect Princess!" roared the twins.

The next morning, as soon as breakfast was over, Grace strode towards the lake. She didn't care how early it was, she was determined to tell Glacia Blizzard exactly what Precious had done.

"Perfect Princess," she muttered under her breath. "Dance thief, more like!"

Normally, Grace would never tell tales – not even on Precious. But this was different. This was cheating, stealing, *robbing* Scarlet of her chance to perform in the show.

Flintheart had been no help. She had stayed away from the auditions and when Grace reported what had happened, the stern skating teacher just sniffed. "Glacia Blizzard made it clear she would make her own choice without any assistance from me."

So that left Grace on her own. Izumi had to go to the Sewing Tower to work on yet more costumes. Visalotta had a piano lesson and although Scarlet was feeling a little better, she was still in sickbay.

"Perhaps it was a mistake," Scarlet had said when she heard that Precious had performed her dance. "I'm sure she didn't mean to copy me quite so exactly." It was typical of Scarlet never to think the worst of anybody, but her eyes had filled up with tears all the same.

Precious won't get away with this, thought Grace, coming to a stop outside the pavilion and staring up at the cold front door. The great, glassy ice walls seemed to tower above her like a fortress. Before she could even stretch out her hand, the door opened with the same sound of breaking ice that Grace remembered from her last visit.

"Ah, it's you. I thought it might be," said old Miss Wintermore, swinging the door wide open and shuffling to one side. "Come in."

Grace stepped into the huge domed hallway.

"I'd tell you not to let the cold in," chuckled Miss Wintermore, shutting the door, "but its the heat we worry about in here." She pointed to the icy walls as if to explain her joke.

"Yes." Grace laughed. "I see that." Her words echoed around the dome. *I see that... I see that... I see that...*

"Wow! It's like a magic cave," Grace said. *Magic cave...* Her voice came back at her again.

"Some people might find it creepy," shrugged Miss Wintermore.

"I don't," said Grace, delighted. "I think

it's fun." *Think it's fun...* For a moment, she had almost forgotten why she was here.

Miss Wintermore cleared her throat. "How can I help? Or did you come simply to admire our echo?"

That's odd, thought Grace. Miss Wintermore's voice didn't echo back at all. Perhaps she was just talking more quietly.

Grace tried to whisper. "I need to see Glacia Blizzard." *Blizzard... Blizzard...*

"Miss Blizzard will not receive visits from fans today," said Miss Wintermore firmly.

"I'm not a fan," said Grace. *Not a fan... Not a fan...* This seemed to echo louder than anything yet. Grace blushed. "That is, I *am* a fan," she explained. "Of course I am. I mean, I think Glacia is amazing. But that's not why I am here. I need to make a complaint." *Complaint... Complaint...*

"The wrong princess has been chosen to dance..."

"Miss Blizzard will not receive guests nor hear complaints, no matter how serious," said Miss Wintermore, talking over the last of Grace's echoing words. "You will have to come back this evening."

"But—" Grace tried again.

Miss Wintermore rapped her walking stick on the frozen floor. That, at least, made an echo. "Come back after school," she said. "You can tell me what has happened and help me clean the skates."

"Skates?" said Grace *Skates...? Skates...? Skates...?*

Miss Wintermore was already shuffling towards the door, swinging it open for Grace to leave.

CHAPTER TWELVE
The Boot Room

Lessons finished early that afternoon, as the Second Years' riding class had been cancelled because of the snow. It was still daylight as Grace set off towards the pavilion once again. She caught sight of Billy looking eagerly over his stable door as she dashed past.

"I'll visit soon, I promise," she called and he whinnied with delight. Grace groaned. She wished she could stop now. But there were only two days until the ice show. So much time had been wasted already. If she was going to tell Glacia Blizzard how Precious had stolen Scarlet's dance, it had to be tonight.

The fading afternoon sun was glinting off the walls of the ice pavilion as she approached. The door was open and the hunched figure of Miss Wintermore was waiting just inside. "Skates," she said, leading Grace to a small room off the domed hallway and carrying on their conversation as if only a minute, rather than an entire day, had passed. She pointed to row upon row of white skating boots lining the shelves of the room.

"Gosh!" said Grace, impressed.

"A hundred pairs for each Ice Maiden," sighed the old wardrobe mistress, sinking on to a bench. "And they all need cleaning."

"All of them? Surely nobody needs a hundred pairs of skates at once?" said Grace.

"Wear and tear. Different dances, different

skates — that sort of thing," said Miss Wintermore vaguely, waving her hands at the shelves. "All I know is they have to be spick and span in time for the performance on Saturday night and it's me who has to clean them."

"But that's awful," said Grace, looking down at the old lady's gnarled hands. "Don't the Ice Maidens help you?"

"Those feather brains?" Miss Wintermore snorted. "Not likely. Too busy preening themselves."

"Well, I'll help," said Grace. "Just show me what to do." She might not be able to sew costumes like Izumi but surely she could polish some boots. Especially as there was no sign of Glacia Blizzard yet...

"You're very kind," said Miss Wintermore. She showed Grace how to dip a cloth into a pot of white wax and rub it into the soft leather of the skates. "Now, tell me, what is it that you think Miss Blizzard ought to hear?"

"It's about the auditions," said Grace, but before she could begin, Miss Wintermore was stumbling to her feet, glancing up at the little ice window above them.

"It's late," she said, lighting a flickering oil lamp with shaky fingers. "I'll fetch a couple of candles, then we can see what we're doing. You carry on." She pointed to the pot of wax. "I shan't be long."

"All right," Grace called. The old lady's footsteps hurried away, moving surprisingly quickly down the icy corridor. "But I have to be back at school in time for supper."

Grace cleaned four pairs of boots. Then six. There was still no sign of Miss Wintermore.

"Grown-ups!" she sighed, raising her

*⋆⁂⋆⋆ ⫻ ⋆⁂⋆⋆

eyebrows. It was the same at home! Haggle, the hairy herdsman, always asked Grace to help him milk the yaks. Then he'd disappear completely, only coming back once the job was done. "I'll never finish these boots by myself, if that's what Miss Wintermore is hoping," she muttered crossly. "I'd have to stay here all night."

"And we don't want that, do we?" said a soft voice from the doorway.

"Yikes!" Grace leapt in the air, sending the pot of wax spinning across the table. "Who's there?"

"Sorry. Did I startle you?" Glacia Blizzard stepped into the room.

Grace opened her mouth and stared. Close up, the star was even taller than she had imagined. Her white-blonde hair tumbled over her shoulders like an avalanche of snow.

"It's so dark in this room you can hardly

see your own hand," she said, raising her fingers as if to prove the point. Her diamond rings and bracelets flashed icy-white in the lamplight. "Here." She lit three bright candles, which filled the room with light and warmth. "Miss Wintermore sent these. But I must say, I think it's jolly mean of her to leave you working here alone."

"Oh, I don't mind. Not really," said Grace. She wondered how much of her mumbled complaint Glacia Blizzard had heard.

"But you didn't come here just to polish skates, did you?" said Glacia, perching beside Grace on the bench. "You came to tell me I have chosen the wrong princess for my show. . ."

"Yes," said Grace. Then she blushed. "I don't think it should be me," she added quickly. She would hate Glacia to think she was here to win the part for herself.

"Especially after I skated into the reeds like that."

"Quite!" Glacia raised an eyebrow and smiled – but not unkindly. "I suspect this has to do with loyalty," she said. "You are here to fight injustice. To plead for a friend who has been wronged..."

"That's it," said Grace. *Wronged* was the perfect word for what Precious had done to Scarlet. She knew at once that Glacia would understand. She began to explain.

Glacia Blizzard's bright face darkened as Grace spoke. She looked shocked and sad.

"So will you let Scarlet audition?" said Grace. "Will you take the part away from Precious?"

Glacia was silent for a moment, then she sighed. "I cannot do that," she said softly. "There are only two days until the show."

"But Scarlet knows the routine," said

Grace. "She knows it better than Precious. It's *her* dance."

"Precious has already begun working with the Ice Maidens. She has seen how the piece will fit the performance," said Glacia. "A change is not possible, I am afraid."

"Oh." Grace felt her shoulders slump. She should have known it would be too late. If only she had been able to talk to Glacia Blizzard this morning. Why did the star always have to hide herself away all day?

"Isn't there anything you can do?" Grace asked.

"The solo dance is a small piece. Five minutes at most," said Glacia. "It is not the most important thing."

"Oh." Grace scratched her head. If the solo wasn't important, then what was?

"You should not be angry with your cousin – you should feel sorry for her," said Glacia. "She believed she had to steal someone else's ideas and pretend they were her own. For this she should be pitied."

Grace thought for a moment. It was sad, in a way, that Precious felt she had to copy Scarlet's dance rather than using her own.

"But Scarlet still lost her chance to perform," she said.

"This time, yes. But Scarlet clearly has a shining talent," said Glacia. "That is the important thing. You should celebrate that and be proud. Imagination can never be stolen."

"You're right," Grace smiled. It was such a shame Scarlet would not get to dance with Glacia Blizzard, but she knew that the famous skater was right. Scarlet was far more creative than Precious would ever be.

"You had better be getting back to school now," said Glacia, glancing at her watch.

Grace saw that, instead of numbers, it had a picture of the sun and the moon. One half of the clock face was black, the other gold.

"Pretty, isn't it?" said Glacia, brightly. "But you really should hurry. I don't want you getting in trouble with *Flintheart* – is that what you call her?"

"Fairy Godmother Flint, yes," smiled Grace. "Shall I say goodbye to Miss Wintermore before I go?" It seemed rude to leave without speaking to the wardrobe mistress.

"Goodness, no." Glacia threw back her head and laughed as if Grace had said something very funny. "Old ladies need their sleep. You won't see Miss Wintermore until first light tomorrow."

"Really?" Grace was surprised. Although it was dark outside, it was still early. Grace hadn't even had her supper. It seemed odd that the wardrobe mistress had just disappeared. The pavilion was strange in that way, she thought to herself. One minute Miss Wintermore was here – the next it was Glacia Blizzard. And there was no sign of the Ice Maidens.

"Shall I come back tomorrow?" Grace asked. Perhaps Miss Wintermore would be back by then. "I can finish cleaning the skates."

"That would be wonderful." Glacia took hold of Grace's hand and squeezed it kindly. Grace shivered in surprise. A chilly tremor ran up her arm as if she had plunged it into snow.

"Sorry, I should have warned you," smiled Glacia. "My hands are as cold as ice."

CHAPTER THIRTEEN
Back to the Boot Room

Next morning, Scarlet came down to the Second-Year common room wrapped up in her dressing gown. She took the news that she wouldn't be able to audition much better than Grace had expected.

"I don't think old Pom would have let me anyway," she said, blowing her nose on a white lace handkerchief. "She's allowed me out of bed for a while, but she's forbidden me to go outside in the snow."

"I don't see what all the fuss is about,"

said Precious, who was sitting in the best chair, right beside the fire. "I'm going to dance in the show and that's all there is to it." She stood up before anyone could argue. "Now, if you'll excuse me, I have a costume fitting to go to in the ice pavilion." She flounced out of the room.

"I'd better go too," sighed Grace. "I told Miss Wintermore I'd finish cleaning the skates."

"I'll help Izumi with her sewing," said Scarlet, moving closer to the fire. "She's just been given a whole lot of new feathers for the Ice Maidens' cloaks."

"Keep warm!" called Grace.

By the time Grace arrived at the pavilion, Precious was wearing her costume. It looked stunning – Izumi had been up half the night sewing sequins on the hem. The clever, artistic princess had even added her own design of tiny snowflakes around the collar.

"It's a good fit," said Miss Wintermore. "And pretty work." She nodded at Grace. "You can tell your friend she has done well."

"I will," said Grace. She knew how pleased Izumi would be.

"Pale blue suits me perfectly. It brings out my eyes," said Precious, twirling in front of the mirror so that the soft gossamer of the fairy costume fluttered around her. Grace hated to admit it, but she did look gorgeous.

"I think I need more sequins though," sighed Precious. "I'll tell Izumi to sew them on."

"Don't you dare. Izumi has quite enough work as it is. And so do I," said Grace, desperate to get away from her preening cousin. "Shall I carry on cleaning the skates for you, Miss Wintermore?"

"Thank you, my dear," the old lady smiled. There was no sign of Glacia Blizzard this morning. Grace had hoped she would get a chance to meet the star up close again. In truth, that was part of the reason she had come. She certainly wasn't looking forward to cleaning rows and rows of skates.

"Precious will join you in the boot room in a moment," said Miss Wintermore. "Just as soon as she has changed out of her costume."

"Me?" Precious looked horrified. "I'm not cleaning other people's skates. I am a solo performer," she cried. "I am a star!"

"Perhaps," sniffed Miss Wintermore. "But you can clean your own skates, I'm sure." She pointed to a smear of dirt beside the sequin P.P.

"This is so unfair," Precious wailed.

Grace smiled to herself and set off towards the boot room. Precious probably hadn't picked up a cleaning rag in her whole life. She was the sort of princess who never made her own bed. Even if she dropped a tissue, Precious expected a maid to pick it up and throw it away for her. "This should be fun," giggled Grace.

Five minutes later, Precious arrived wearing her school uniform and a furious frown. "Wait till Daddy hears about this," she whined, thumping her skates down on the bench. "I am a princess and a performer, not a servant..."

"Oh, put a sock in it," sighed Grace. "Everyone has to help if we want this show to be a success. Think how much hard work Izumi has done on the costumes. She practically designed your frost fairy costume all by herself. Scarlet is busy sewing today too, even though she's still sick. Here," she said, reaching behind her and grabbing a pair of skates from the shelf, "you can clean one extra pair at least."

"But..." Precious made a strange whimpering sound and grabbed Grace's arm.

"Oh, just do it." Grace had had enough now.

Precious was still pulling on her sleeve. "Look!"

"What?" Grace turned and glanced down. The skates she had grabbed and put in front of Precious were not white like the others. They were silver ... and they were glowing softly like the moon on a dark winter night.

CHAPTER FOURTEEN
The Silver Skates

Precious and Grace had not held hands since they were two years old. But the cousins grasped each other now, staring in wonder at the gleaming skates.

"They're beautiful," said Grace.

"I want them!" Precious dropped Grace's hand and lunged for the boots.

"Don't!" Grace leapt in front of Precious, protecting the skates as if they were a fragile dragon's egg in a nest. "We shouldn't even have touched them," she said. "They look so ... magical." It was the only word she could think of to describe the shimmering silver skates.

"Valuable, more like it," said Precious. "They must be worth a fortune." She swung round on the bench and stuck out her foot. "Give them to me," she ordered. "I'm going to try them on."

"They won't fit you," said Grace. "Look." Without thinking, she leant forward and touched the skates. The soft, silvery leather felt warm, like when a friend takes your hand in the snow. "Your feet are too small," said Grace, forcing herself to let go of the leather.

Precious's feet were slim and narrow. Grace realized with a jolt that the skates would be much more likely to fit her instead. She longed to try them on. What harm could it do? Precious was holding the right boot. Grace grabbed the left.

"One foot each," she said quickly. "We'll just slip them on. Then we'll put them back."

But, before they could even bend down, the door to the boot room swung open and Miss Wintermore appeared. Her crooked old back straightened in fury. She seemed as tall as Glacia Blizzard now. Her pale eyes were blazing bright with rage.

"Who said you could touch those skates?" she roared.

"Grace touched them first," squealed Precious. "She got them down from the shelf."

"I – I didn't think they were special," said Grace. She looked at the shining skates and realized what a stupid thing this was to say. "I mean, I can see they are special now, of course. But when I first picked them up …

they were just on the shelf … I…"

"An honest mistake," said Miss Wintermore, in a gentler tone. She seemed tired and stooped again. She reached forward and lifted the skates into her arms. "You are right though, they are special. Very special."

The old wardrobe mistress cradled the skates as if they held a secret she didn't ever want to let go. A secret or a memory…

Grace glanced down at the old lady's own twisted feet. She was wearing a pair of wide black boots. "Oh!" Miss Wintermore had big feet – just like Grace's own. "They're yours, aren't they?" she said. "You wore the skates when you were younger."

"Mine?" The old lady threw back her head and laughed in a way that reminded Grace of someone she had seen before. "They are not mine, my dear. They never were. What would I want with silver skates?"

"They belong to Glacia Blizzard, of course," said Precious, rolling her eyes as if Grace was stupid. "Anyone can see that."

"You're right. They do belong to Miss Blizzard," said the old lady, placing the skates back on the high shelf. Grace saw now that they were lying on a special blue silk cushion. "She wore them the very first time she performed on ice as a young girl."

"And it's my first performance tomorrow night," said Precious. "So I should wear them too." She clicked her fingers at Miss Wintermore. "Call Glacia Blizzard now! I need to have those skates."

Grace blushed but Miss Wintermore took no notice of Precious's high and mighty tone. "Miss Blizzard will not be available until this evening," she said calmly. "She will see you for a rehearsal on the ice at dusk. Until then, I suggest you take those –"

she pointed a bent finger at Precious's own initialled skates "– and go and practise on the lake."

"Fine!" Precious stomped to the door. "Wait till I tell Glacia how you've treated me. She'll let me wear the skates, I know she will. I'm her star performer."

"Oh dear," smiled Miss Wintermore as Precious stormed away down the icy corridor. "I think Princess Precious is used to getting her own way…"

Grace smiled and picked up her rag. She had only been polishing for a moment before she glanced over her shoulder at the silver skates. She couldn't help it. She had to look at them again. The spoilt way Precious had behaved was dreadful, but Grace understood how much she wanted the skates. Grace wanted them too. She had never wanted anything so much – except a unicorn, of course. It was all she could do not to reach up and touch them.

"The silver skates wouldn't even fit Precious," she muttered. "They'd be far too big."

"Do you know what?" said Miss Wintermore, glancing down at Grace's big feet sticking out from under the bench. "I think you might be right."

CHAPTER FIFTEEN
A Terrible Tantrum

The next day passed in a whirl of suspense and expectation as every princess in the school looked forward to the show that night. Scarlet's temperature dropped and Fairy Godmother Pom agreed she could join the audience so long as she wrapped up warm. Grace scrubbed and polished another fifty pairs of ice skates. Izumi sewed two hundred sequins. And Precious forced the twins to brush her hair a thousand times, while she boasted about her part in the show. All this time, she was hardly ever seen out on the ice rehearsing.

At last, the sun sank low in the sky. With just three hours until the start of the performance, the dormitories of Tall Towers were buzzing with excitement. The princesses dashed up and down stairs borrowing ribbons and brooches, trying on tiaras and choosing their fanciest outfits to wear for the big event.

The twins had changed thirteen times already. They ran in and out of every Second Year dorm wearing their latest choice – matching peach-coloured polka-dot frocks with frilly ruffles around their necks like performing poodles.

"What do you think? How adorable do we look?" they asked. But they never stayed long enough to hear the answer.

"Anyone ready to see outfit fourteen?" they cried.

Even Grace had made an effort to look smart. She brushed her hair for five whole minutes and tied her unusually neat plaits with pretty white bows. Normally, she would have asked her friends to help her but this evening she was on her own in the little attic dorm. Scarlet was in sickbay having a hot lemon, ginger and cinnamon tea, which Fairy Godmother Pom had insisted she should drink before going out in the cold, and Izumi had made one last trip to the Sewing Tower to sew an extra ring of sequins around the edge of Precious's fairy wings.

Grace paced round and round, glancing out the window as the red glow of the sinking sun faded away and the sky turned inky black. The excitement was too much.

She felt like a knight's charger tied up before a joust.

The twins poked their heads around the door in a swirl of custard-yellow frocks. "These are definitely the ones, don't you think?" they squealed, then thundered away before Grace could answer.

"I can't stand this a moment longer," groaned Grace, ripping a sheet of paper from the back of her history of royal families exercise book.

MEET YOU AT THE LAKE, she scribbled. Then she clipped the note to the mirror with one of Scarlet's hair grips. Her friends were sure to notice it there.

Grace grabbed her big hairy Cragland coat. She wrapped a woolly scarf around her neck and dashed down the stairs, almost colliding with the twins. They must have nearly run out of outfits, as they were

wearing matching white, fluffy polar bear fancy dress costumes.

"I'm just not sure," sighed Trinket.

"Not sure at all," agreed Truffle.

"You look perfect," grinned Grace, squeezing past them. "Polar bears love the snow!"

She skidded out of the door into the dark, frosty gardens. Precious had been called for a last-minute rehearsal and Grace was desperate to see if Glacia Blizzard or any of the Ice Maidens were on the lake too.

"Oh!" Grace gasped with wonder as she slithered to a stop at the edge of the lake. Golden chairs lined the snowy banks for the audience to sit on. The ice shone like a magic mirror, as if it had been polished with a cloth. A hundred torches were lit, flames leaping high into the dark sky. In the middle of the rink, the twelve silent Ice Maidens perfected a fast spinning routine, swooping soundlessly in circles, their pale feathered practice skirts fluttering in the breeze, their arms stretched out towards each other like beautiful sweeping wings.

Grace shivered. The silence was almost eerie. She realized that in all the times she had come to the lake she had never heard any of the Ice Maidens speak. The only sound was Precious's voice as it rang across the ice.

"How much longer is this going to take?" she moaned as she rehearsed with Glacia Blizzard in front of the pavilion. "I'm freezing cold."

"I am sorry you are chilly, Young Majesty," said Glacia, taking off her shawl and wrapping it around Precious's shoulders. "But we would have been finished by now if you hadn't been an hour late for rehearsal. As it is, we do not have many minutes before the show."

Grace was shocked. Every Tall Towers princess knew how important it was to be on time for rehearsals. She slipped silently under the frozen branches of a weeping willow tree so she could watch the skaters without disturbing anyone by being seen.

"It's not my fault I was late. I had to make sure my hair was perfect," sighed Precious.

"The only thing that matters is how you will dance tonight," said Glacia Blizzard, gently lifting Precious's elbows. "Hold your arms higher. Like this – as if you are a fairy borne aloft by the winter wind."

"Fine!" huffed Precious. She stuck her arms right up by her ears and spun furiously away.

"A little lower than that, Young Majesty,"

said Glacia Blizzard patiently, but Precious kicked at the ice.

"You just told me to put them higher. I knew it would look stupid," she snapped.

Grace ducked further into the shadows of the tree. How could Precious be so rude? She knew that if Scarlet was well enough, she would have given anything to have a one-to-one lesson with Glacia on the ice. Grace would have loved it too, if only she didn't think she'd fall flat on her bottom.

You never know, she thought, *Glacia might even be able to teach me to spin on my skates.*

"I can't do it!" Precious moaned. "It's not my arms I'm worried about anyway. It's my feet. I can barely move them. These skates are far too small."

Grace peered through the branches of the willow tree. Precious was wearing her brand-new P.P.-initialled skating boots. They had arrived only a few days earlier and had fitted perfectly then.

"Ouch!" Precious was hobbling about the ice as if her feet were caught in a trap. "My toes are going to be stunted for ever by these stupid skates."

"Perhaps we can lend you a larger pair," sighed Glacia, gesturing towards the pavilion. Grace could see that Glacia Blizzard's patience was beginning to run out. "Do you need to change now, Princess Precious, or can we rehearse first?"

"Right now," said Precious. "And I want to wear the silver skates."

"Of course!" breathed Grace. She should have guessed. There was nothing wrong with Precious's skates at all. She just wanted to wear Glacia's shimmering silver ones instead. That was what all this sulking was about.

Glacia Blizzard folded her arms. "You

cannot just wear the silver skates, Princess Precious," she said firmly. "You must earn them first."

"But I want them!" Precious threw herself down on the ice. "My daddy will make you give them to me!"

"You are wasting my time," said Glacia, her voice was icy with rage. "I'm going to count to three. If you have not stood up by then, you will not perform tonight. One..."

"I want the skates!" roared Precious.

"Two..."

Grace's heart was thumping in her chest. Still Precious did not stand up.

"Three," said Glacia Blizzard. "You have lost your chance. You will not dance in my show."

"But..." Precious staggered to her feet at last. "You can't do that."

Grace couldn't believe it. Had Precious really thrown away the chance to appear in Glacia Blizzard's ice show?

"You won't find anyone else now, not at such short notice," Precious wailed, grabbing the hem of Glacia's cloak. "Nobody can dance as brilliantly as me."

If only Scarlet were well enough, thought Grace. *This would be her chance. She wouldn't even need to rehearse. She could just step straight on to the ice.*

But Glacia Blizzard had turned away and was skating straight towards the weeping willow tree. It was almost as if she knew somebody was hiding there.

"Don't worry, Princess Precious," she said. "I already have another skater in mind for the show."

Grace froze. Surely Glacia would sweep straight past?

But the famous skater skidded to a stop and parted the frozen leaves as if they were curtains on a stage.

"Come out, Princess Grace," she called. "I want you to skate in my show."

CHAPTER SIXTEEN
The New Dancer

Grace opened and closed her mouth in disbelief. "You want me to dance in the show?"

"Of course," said Glacia kindly. "You have hidden talents which I would like the whole school to see."

Hidden talents? The only thing Grace was any good at was falling over... Oh, and unicorn riding, but she could hardly take Billy out on the ice. "If Precious isn't going to perform, then it should be Scarlet," she said. "I know you haven't seen her skate properly. But she's wonderful. She would be far better than me. She'd be better than anybody in the whole school."

"Your loyalty to your friend is admirable," Glacia smiled. "But Scarlet is not well. So that is the end of that."

"But..." Grace couldn't make sense of anything that was going on. Had Glacia Blizzard really chosen her to skate in front of the whole school? Just thinking about it made Grace feel as if slippery eels were wriggling inside her tummy.

Grace glanced over her shoulder. Precious had stormed away and was sprawled on a bench at the edge of the lake. She was furiously kicking her feet so that splinters of wood flew into the air.

"Couldn't you give Precious one last chance?" she asked Glacia.

But the famous skater shook her head. "I simply cannot work with a princess as spoilt as Precious. She cares nothing for skating, only for herself."

"You won't get away with this, Glacia Blizzard," Precious roared. "I'm a princess! You should obey me! I'll tell Lady DuLac ... I'll tell Fairy Godmother Flint ... I'll tell my daddy..."

"As I have already made quite clear," said Glacia, frostily, "Grace is my chosen skater now." She turned and began to glide away towards the Ice Maidens. "If you will excuse me, I must practise some of my own routines in the last few minutes we have left."

"Wait," Grace ran around the edge of the lake, trying to catch up with her. "Don't I need to rehearse?"

"Why bother?" sneered Precious. "A

whole year of rehearsals wouldn't help you get any better, Grace."

"Go stick your head in a snow drift!" said Grace. All sympathy for her cousin was gone. She had got everything she deserved.

"You'll be fine." Glacia Blizzard turned to Grace with her brightest smile. "Have faith in yourself."

"But I don't even have a routine," stammered Grace. "Precious is right. I am pretty hopeless." Already, the faint sound of voices was echoing from the path. Some of the princesses must be making their way towards the lake to take their places in the audience. "There's less than half an hour to go!" said Grace, clutching her tummy.

"Don't worry." Glacia swept over and took Grace by the hands. "I will be with you every step of the way. We can skate together."

"You mean, I'll just have to copy what you do?" asked Grace.

"Exactly. Remember those hidden talents, Princess Grace. You are strong and brave," Glacia called as she swirled away. "Just ask Izumi to let down the hem on Precious's fairy costume for you and everything else will be fine."

Everything except for the fact that I can barely skate, thought Grace.

CHAPTER SEVENTEEN
Snatching the Skates

Grace watched as Glacia Blizzard began her last-minute rehearsals with the Ice Maidens on the far side of the lake.

They were spinning so high, it looked almost as if they had wings.

"I hope Glacia doesn't want me to skate like that," shivered Grace. She wished she could run away. But it was too late now. The excited voices coming from the garden were growing louder.

A moment later, Scarlet and Izumi

appeared in the torchlight at the edge of the lake.

"There you are." Scarlet sneezed. She was wrapped up like a woolly parcel, wearing a knitted bobble hat pulled over her ears and clutching a hot-water bottle, which Old Pom must have insisted on before letting her out.

"I've got so much to tell you," cried Grace. She glanced over her shoulder and saw that the bench behind her was empty. "Have you seen Precious?" she asked. Perhaps her friends knew everything already. If her cousin had stormed back to school, she would have been sure to pass them on the path.

"No sign of Precious," said Izumi. "But we did see the note you left on the mirror."

"You were lucky to get out when

you did," added Scarlet. "Flintheart says everyone is thoroughly overexcited. She has made the whole school line up silently in the Great Hall. Even the Sixth Formers. Nobody is going to be allowed down here until five minutes before the start of the show."

"She only let us out because I said you and Scarlet would help me hang up the skating dresses," said Izumi, lifting a pile of costumes in her outstretched arms. "I thought you could save yourselves a couple of good seats." She nodded towards the front row. "I don't think I'll need one. I'll be too busy backstage."

"But that's just it," said Grace as the two girls chattered excitedly. "I won't need a seat either. Precious has lost her part. I am going to skate in the show."

"You?" The chattering stopped. Her

friends sounded shocked. They were both too kind to say anything, but the look of surprise on their faces said it all.

"I know! It's crazy," Grace groaned. She told them everything that had happened. "It really was Precious's fault," she explained. "She was being so spoilt about the silver skates. But I still don't know why Glacia asked *me* to replace her. It's as if she doesn't even remember my terrible audition. Do you think she might have me confused with somebody else?"

"I'm sure Glacia must know what she's doing," said Scarlet, biting her lip. Even though she was the most loyal friend in the whole world, Grace didn't think she sounded very sure.

"Glacia Blizzard can't have you confused with anyone else," said Izumi.

"Of course not," agreed Scarlet, sounding much more certain. "After all, Grace, you are totally unique!"

Grace smiled. Her friends were trying their best to make her feel better, and she was going to need all the support she could get. She was pretty sure Precious wouldn't speak to her ever again.

"Where can she have got to?" she wondered. Glacia and the Ice Maidens were still practising at far end of the lake. She glanced over her other shoulder at the pavilion. A flickering lamp from the little boot-room window made a perfect, pale rectangle of light on the ice.

"Oh no! Precious is in the pavilion," she cried, bumping into Izumi and sending the costumes flying. "Sorry!" She was already dashing away.

Although Glacia Blizzard had forbidden it, Grace knew that her spoilt cousin never took no for an answer. "I have to stop Precious," she called. "I think she's going to steal the skates."

As Grace sped closer, she saw that the huge

ice door to the pavilion was open wide.

"Precious?" she called, skidding through the door. "Precious, are you here?"

Precious...? The hallway echoed but there was no sign of her cousin. Grace flew through the hall, half expecting to see Miss Wintermore... But there was no one in sight.

She rushed towards the boot room and flung open the door.

Sure enough, Precious was reaching up to grab the silver skates from the highest shelf.

"Put them back," cried Grace as Precious hid the shimmering boots under her white fur cape.

"Get lost!" Precious spun around. "Keep your nose out of my business."

"But the skates aren't yours," said Grace, trying to catch her breath. "You have to put them back. What if Glacia needs them for the show?"

"I don't care!" Precious flicked her shining hair. "I want them. Daddy will pay for them if he has to."

"I don't think it works like that," said Grace. Precious always believed that anything could be bought with money. "The skates are special."

Precious tried to barge past Grace in the doorway.

"Stop!" Grace stretched out her hand and grabbed hold of the left boot which was poking out from under her cousin's cloak. As her fingers clasped the silver leather she felt a tingle run down her spine. More than ever, she understood why Precious wanted to steal the skates and keep them for herself. But Grace knew it was wrong.

"We have to put them back," she said quickly. The skates were tied together by the laces. The girls had one boot each, pulling in opposite directions.

"Give them to me!" howled Precious, crying with rage and fury. "*Please.*" She was almost begging now.

"I'm sorry. I can't," said Grace. "I won't. It's not right." *I might be clumsy*, she thought, *but I'm stronger than Precious – and taller too.* She lifted her arm high in the air and pulled as hard as she could.

"What's going on?" Grace heard a sharp voice in the domed hallway outside. For a moment she thought it was Miss Wintermore but, out of the corner of her eye, she saw Glacia Blizzard swooping down the corridor towards them. "What are you doing?" Just like Miss Wintermore, Glacia Blizzard's voice didn't echo in the icy dome either.

Precious looked around. Grace yanked at the skate with one last almighty tug.

"No!" Precious screamed.

Grace toppled over backwards with both silver skates clutched tightly in her arms. "Got them!" she breathed.

"Well done," smiled Glacia Blizzard,

scooping the skates out of Grace's hand. "Now please leave the pavilion, Princess Precious. It is time for the show."

"Wait till my daddy hears about this!" Precious barged past the famous skater. "You'll never be invited to do any royal performances ever again. He knows all the most important kings and queens in the world. How can you do this to me?" she screamed. "How can you give my starring role to someone as hopeless as Princess Disgrace?"

Princess Disgrace... The words echoed around the icy dome as Precious stormed out of the pavilion.

CHAPTER EIGHTEEN
The Snow Fairy Costume

With the silver skates safely returned, Izumi arrived with the costumes and Glacia Blizzard left Grace to get ready for the show.

"Take no notice of Precious. I bet she's so jealous she won't even stay and watch," said Izumi.

"At least that'll be one less person in the audience," said Grace, trying to smile.

But, two minutes later, Scarlet popped her head round the door to wish Grace good luck. "Precious just barged three of the smallest First Years out of the way, so she and the twins could get seats in the front row," she sighed.

"That's all I need!" said Grace. Her heart was beating so hard she felt as if someone was swinging a hammer inside her chest.

"You'll be wonderful! I'll keep my fingers crossed for you." Scarlet disappeared to take her own seat, but not before Grace saw she was biting her lip again.

"I don't even know what I'm doing," she whispered, as Izumi pulled the delicate snow fairy costume over her head.

"Just do your best," said Izumi, "you can't do more than that." But Grace could feel her friend's fingers shaking as she fastened the tiny pearl buttons down her back.

Around them the Ice Maidens flittered and fluttered with last-minute preparations. They still didn't say a word. The only sound was the icy jingle of sequins on their snowy feather-white costumes. Grace was so nervous, she wanted to giggle. But the silent skaters looked so serious, she didn't dare.

"Probably concentrating. Getting in the zone," she whispered as Izumi knelt and tugged at the hem of the fairy costume.

"You might get in the zone yourself, if you stopped jiggling from foot to foot," Izumi said through a mouthful of pins.

"Sorry!" Grace tried her best to stand still. Poor Izumi had worked like a whirlwind to finish the costume in time. She'd had to let the hem down at least five centimetres from the height it had been for Precious.

"What do you think?" Izumi spun Grace round so that she could see her reflection in a full-length mirror of shining ice.

"Gosh..." Grace blinked. The dress was sprinkled from head to toe with frosted snowflake sequins as if the winter wind had swirled past her in a glittering storm. The soft fabric shimmered, shifting from pale blue to silver like a frozen mountain stream. "I can't believe you made this. Thank you, Izumi," she said. "I look..."

"Beautiful!" said Glacia Blizzard, appearing suddenly behind her and stepping up to the mirror so that they were reflected side by side. The famous skater's dress was the same icy-blue colour but, instead of sequins, her costume shimmered with shards of real ice.

"You'll have fairy wings too, of course," said Izumi, slipping delicate hoops of silver netting over Grace's shoulder.

"Perfect! You remind me of the first time I skated in a show," smiled Glacia. "We look quite similar, don't you think?"

Grace blushed. "It's just because we're both tall," she said. Surely that was the

only thing she truly had in common with the glamorous ice dancer. Without the beautiful costumes, they were as opposite as a shimmering diamond and a stick of wood, Grace thought.

"You seem different from the other pupils here at Tall Towers," said Glacia gently.

"It's true," laughed Grace. "Flintheart – I mean Fairy Godmother Flint – is always telling me how different I am ... and not usually in a good way!" She looked at Izumi to back this up. "Even though I am in the Second Year now, I'm forever getting things wrong. Precious says I'll never learn to be a proper princess. She thinks I shouldn't be at the school at all..." Grace trailed off, realizing she had said too much. Glacia Blizzard didn't want to know all this – especially now she had chosen her to dance in the show.

But the ice star nodded. "Tell me, what do you see when you look in that mirror now?"

"Er ... a very tall frost fairy," laughed Grace.

Izumi giggled, but Glacia Blizzard frowned. "What I see is a perfect princess," she said. "When you go out on that ice tonight, every girl in the school will wish they could be *you*."

For once, Grace was lost for words. "Thank you!" she whispered. Could it be true? Could she really be a perfect princess, even if it was only for one night, even if she had knobbly knees and turned-out feet? Grace glanced down. One big toe was already poking out of the spider's-web-thin stockings Izumi had given her just five minutes before.

"Oh no!" Grace's heart sank. She had

forgotten there was still one part of the costume left to go. She glanced over at the terrible clumpy brown skates. She would never look like a gentle fairy – the skates were more like something a thundering mountain troll might wear. She wished there was a white pair she could use, but she had bigger feet than any other princess in the school and none of the Ice Maidens' skates would fit her. Their feet were as tiny as a bird's.

"I know what you need." Glacia Blizzard seemed to read her mind. "The silver skates would look wonderful with your costume, wouldn't they?"

"The silver skates?" Grace goggled. "*Your* silver skates?" Surely Glacia didn't mean that she could borrow those?

But the famous skater was already reaching towards the shelf.

"They will be perfect," she said.

"But..." Grace's head was spinning like a kaleidoscope. "I thought nobody was allowed to wear them. When Precious asked, you said no."

"Precious did not deserve them," said Glacia, laying her hand on Grace's arm. "You rescued them from her." She had slipped off her white leather gloves and Grace felt a shiver of cold run across her skin.

"The skates are like that," said Glacia. "They bring out the best in people... Or they bring out the worst." She held up the shimmering silver boots so that they glistened like diamonds in the flickering lamplight.

"They really do sparkle like the stars," gasped Izumi, who had never seen them close up until now.

Glacia Blizzard seemed lost in a dream,

as if she too was transfixed by the skates. At last, she shook her head and held them towards Grace.

"Go on! Try them," she said. "I am certain they will be a perfect fit."

CHAPTER NINETEEN
The Show Begins

Glacia Blizzard knelt down. Either she didn't notice Grace's big toe poking out from hole in her stockings or she was too polite to mention it. She slipped the silver skates on to Grace's feet.

"How do they feel?" she asked.

Grace wiggled her toes. "Perfect!" she grinned. The skates could have been made for her, they fitted so well.

As she stood up, her soles began to tingle as if the skates were full of popping candy fizzing beneath her feet. It felt ticklish and she might have giggled if it wasn't for the roar of the audience outside. Her feet felt as if they were on fire.

"It's just excitement ... or nerves," she told herself, holding on to Izumi's shoulder for support.

"Ready?" Glacia Blizzard gave her one last smile. "Show time!" she said. Then she turned and skated away across the polished floor of the pavilion. Reaching the door, she threw back her shoulders and straightened the sharp crown of shining icicles on her head. All at once, she seemed like a true snow queen.

"See you on the ice, Princess Grace. You'll be perfect," she said as the huge front door was flung open and a cheer went up from the crowd outside.

The Ice Maidens skated after her.

"Good luck!" whispered Grace. But they were as poised and silent as ever.

"I don't suppose we'd hear even if they did answer," said Grace, still holding tight to Izumi's shoulder as she wobbled on the skates. The noise from outside was deafening. Grace wagged her finger. "*What an un-princess-like hullabaloo*," she scolded.

"Brilliant! You've got Flintheart perfectly," Izumi laughed.

Grace peeped out of the pavilion door and caught sight of the strict teacher in the very front row. She was leaning forward, her half-moon glasses perched on the end of her pointy nose, looking just as desperate as everyone else for the long-awaited show to begin.

Grace could see Precious scowling. Scarlet was there too, sitting between Visalotta and Fairy Godmother Pom. She was wrapped up in three more scarves and an extra shawl which the kind old seamstress must have insisted on. Even amongst all those layers, Grace could see her eyes were wide with excitement . . . and she was still biting her lip.

The audience fell quiet at last as Glacia Blizzard took her place on the centre of the rink. She stood, still as a statue.

"We'll have a great view from here, Izumi," whispered Grace, edging around the pavilion door. "I can watch the whole show, until it's time for my bit."

"Stay tucked behind the pillars," warned Izumi, grabbing Grace's arm and pulling her out of sight.

The two friends watched in delight as ice-blue flames sprung to life all around the edge of the frozen stage. The winter darkness was filled with a strange, pale, haunting light. Somewhere out of the gloom came the clear, crisp sound of violins.

"I didn't even know there was an orchestra," said Grace.

Slowly – so slowly that, at first, it appeared she was frozen like ice – Glacia Blizzard began to move. First her fingers... Then her arms... It was as if she was coming to life after a long winter sleep. Then ... *whoosh!* She leapt into the air and spun eight times high above the ice.

"Hooray! Bravo!" The crowd went wild.

"Whoopee!" Grace cheered too.

"Shh!" Izumi smiled and put her finger to her lips. Every now and then, she dashed into the pavilion to bring little pieces of costume that were needed in the show.

Glacia Blizzard whirled across the rink. She was wearing a simple pair of plain white skates – since Grace had the silver ones – and they barely seemed to touch the ice.

She swerved and spun and pirouetted in and out of the dancing Ice Maidens. Together they made shapes like Jack Frost on a frozen window – first a feather, then a fern leaf, now a snowflake.

Glacia Blizzard's dance showed a young snow queen, lost and left alone in a land of endless winter. There were no words, of course, but the story was as clear to Grace as if she had read it in a book. Glacia made

everything so real. The howling wind which blew her far away from home. The long trek through a frozen forest. The hopeless search for food. Grace wept as Glacia trembled with exhaustion and giggled with delight when she met a wolf cub, played by one of the Ice Maidens in a painted mask.

"Isn't it brilliant?" she said, turning to Izumi. "I feel as if I'm with Glacia all the way and we're lost in a magical snowy world."

"Just don't get too lost," hissed Izumi. She grabbed the wolf mask from an Ice Maiden and put it to one side. "You're on in two minutes."

"Two minutes? Is that all?" Grace felt her tummy drop like a yo-yo on a broken string.

"One minute now," said Izumi, bending down to check Grace's laces were tied up extra tight. "We don't want you tripping over those!" she grinned. "Ready?'

Grace nodded. She watched as the Ice Maidens withdrew to the edge of the rink. She knew they would return after her routine, dressed in new costumes to show the winter thaw was on its way. That's why her dance was there. It allowed time for them to change.

"I feel sick," she gulped. She had been so wrapped up in watching the show, she had almost forgotten about her own performance.

"I'll fall flat on my face, I know I will."

"Rubbish!" Izumi pushed her gently forward. "You'll be brilliant. Glacia is right – you're a proper princess and you're going to make everyone at Tall Towers proud!"

Grace wobbled on to the ice. Out of the corner of her eye, she saw Scarlet jump to her feet and cheer. All the other Second Years leapt up too. Even the twins. Only Precious stayed sitting down. She looked so sour she might have swallowed a whole basket of lemons.

Suddenly, she spotted Grace's silver skates. "That's so unfair!" she cried, leaping to her feet so fast now that she hit one of the twins in the nose. "Grace can't wear those skates! They should have been mine."

"Shhh!" Flintheart waved her arms, trying to quieten Precious down.

"Concentrate!" Grace told herself as she

skated steadily onwards. Glacia Blizzard was waiting for her in the middle of the rink. All the other skaters were gone. Even Izumi was inside the pavilion, helping the Ice Maidens with their costume change.

Grace's ankles ached with tension. *At least I haven't fallen over yet,* she thought. *All I have to do is make it to Glacia Blizzard and then she'll take my hand.*

But first she had to greet the headmistress, sitting in the centre of the front row. Grace stopped directly in front of Lady DuLac and curtsied perfectly.

"Wow! I've never managed a curtsy as neat as that before," she muttered. Grace thought she was whispering under her breath. But, on the still of the ice, the audience heard every word and broke into fits of laughter – Grace's wobbly curtsies were famous throughout the school. Only

Flintheart wasn't laughing – and Precious, who was shaking her fist with furious rage.

"Well done!" Lady DuLac nodded, and her eyes twinkled with encouragement.

Grace skated on. The curtsy had given her new courage. Her feet felt so light in the skates, and for once they were actually doing what she told them too.

Grace lifted her arms high and threw back her head without even the slightest wobble.

"Gosh!" she heard a First Year in the front row gasp. "Princess Grace looks just like Glacia Blizzard."

Perhaps the silver skates will bring me luck, she thought. *Perhaps I really can make everybody at Tall Towers proud of me tonight.*

"Here goes!" She reached towards the famous ice dancer's outstretched hands.

CHAPTER TWENTY
Skating

Glacia Blizzard took hold of Grace's hand.

"Thank you for being in my show tonight," she whispered as she led Grace slowly in a gentle figure of eight. "Don't forget, you have something which many of these other princesses lack."

"Two left feet?" giggled Grace.

But Glacia shook her head. "You may not be as elegant as your friend Scarlet or as creative as Izumi," she said, pulling Grace a little faster across the ice. "You may not be as sure of yourself as Princess Precious. But you have determination and stamina. That is why I have chosen you to help me tonight."

"And you even let me wear the silver skates," beamed Grace. She felt a glow of pride as if the tingles in her feet were filling her whole body with sparks of fire. It was true – she *was* strong. She could ride a unicorn further and faster than anyone else. She had won a joust against fierce knights in shining armour and harnessed an enormous dragon last year. But none of these things had ever made her feel as princessey as she did now, spinning across the ice.

Her long hair was free of its knotty plaits and flowing out behind her. The beautiful fairy costume Izumi had made was as glamorous and sparkly as a ballgown, but most of all, it was the silver skates which made Grace feel like a true princess. For the first time in her life, her long legs seemed to know which way they were supposed to be going and her feet were as light as air. It was as if somebody had waved a magic wand and all her clumsiness had vanished.

Grace held tight to Glacia's hand and glanced down at the glittering skates.

She was leaping and spinning so high, the ice beneath her was a blur.

The crowd were on their feet, cheering her name.

Grace would never have believed that she could skate like this but Glacia Blizzard spun her round, urging her without any words to twist and leap and spin. The only thing Grace could see was the silver shimmer of the dancing skates beneath her.

She had never been any good at ballet or ballroom waltzes. Even simple country reels were usually a disaster. The poor twins had got tied up in ribbons like two pink piglets when Grace had gone the wrong way round the maypole last spring. Perhaps it was because Grace came from the frozen shores of Cragland, but – at last – she had found a way to move… She was good at skating. She was fast and fearless, but nimble too.

"How elegant you are," whispered a voice in her ear, as Glacia twirled her round and then – quite suddenly, without any warning – let her go.

"Dance!" she cried.

Grace didn't even wobble. One, two, three times she spun. Her leg was stretched out behind her like a proper ballet arabesque.

Grace wanted to pinch herself. Perhaps she was dreaming? But she could feel the rush of cold air on her face. She was here, on the lake, in front of the whole school, skating a duet with the most famous and beautiful ice dancer in all the world.

"See," whispered Glacia Blizzard as they criss-crossed past each other on the ice. "You really do deserve your name. You truly are a graceful princess, Grace."

"Thank you!" Grace breathed. She almost thought she was going to wobble. But the skates still held her firm.

"We're moving so fast," she whispered as

they criss-crossed back the other way. The warm feeling inside had spread right up from her toes into her chest. She felt her heart might melt like ice with all its fiery glow.

Feeling as light as a goose feather in the wind, she rose up on to the toe of her skate and began to twirl the other way.

It was only as she was spinning that she saw the crowd. Something strange was happening to the audience. Grace realized they were silent now. There was not a sound, except the winter wind blowing in off the sea. She saw Scarlet reach up her hand. But it was frozen in mid-air as if her fingers had been turned to ice. Flintheart too was as still as cold grey stone.

"What's happening?" gasped Grace. She tried to stop spinning but her feet would not obey.

"Keep dancing," urged Glacia Blizzard. "The show must go on."

"But my friends," said Grace. "The teachers, my headmistress..."

Lady DuLac was leaning forward, her long grey hair like a frozen waterfall around her shoulders. Her face was as white as snow and her pale blue robes had turned to frost.

"They are frozen," gasped Grace.

Precious was caught too, running towards the ice as if she had been trying to push Grace over and grab the silver skates. Her mouth was open in a silent scream of fury. Her arms were raised and her hair, fanned out behind her, was crystallized with sleet.

"They're statues," cried Grace. She tried to dig her heels into the ice but the silver skates just kept on turning.

"Help me!" Grace called out to Glacia Blizzard. "I need to stop skating, but I can't." She spun closer to the star. "We have to do something."

But the famous ice dancer just threw back her head and laughed. "You are doing perfectly, Grace," she grinned. "You are doing all I could ever have asked."

"You don't understand. I want to stop. I need to help my friends." Did Glacia Blizzard still think she was talking about the show? How well she was performing for the crowd? None of that mattered any more. Grace was feeling sick with dizziness. She wished the spinning would cease.

"Don't you see?" cried Grace. "Everyone has turned to solid ice." She looked again at Scarlet, who was cold and white as marble. "All of them, except you and me."

"Exactly!" Glacia skated calmly round her as Grace spun faster than a leaf in the wind. "Brilliant, isn't it? It is all part of my plan."

"Your plan?" Grace used all her strength to spin the other way. For a moment, at least, her dizziness cleared. She lunged forward, gliding across the ice, but she couldn't stop. Her feet went on sliding forward beneath her.

"The skates," she gasped. "It's like they're enchanted. I can't stop skating. My feet will not stand still."

"You will never stop skating now," smiled Glacia. "Not until a hundred hearts freeze over." Grace saw her glance towards the audience, as if counting the rows of girls and teachers who had turned to ice.

There were at least one hundred people here. If not more.

"You did this to them, didn't you?" said

Grace. "You turned them all to ice!"

"Me?" Glacia Blizzard skated backwards across the lake beside her. "I didn't do anything. It was all you, my dear. You did want so very much to wear those skates. And you are right; they are magical. Their enchantment has turned your friends and teachers into ice."

"But how?" Grace felt her feet lift up and she leapt helplessly into the air. "Why?"

"Because I commanded it!" said Glacia with a cold smile. "As you skated, everybody froze. It is as simple as that."

Her voice had once sounded soft and beautiful, but now it hissed and whistled like the frosty wind.

At last, Grace understood. "You are a witch!" she gasped. A chill of fear ran down her aching spine. "And I have helped you do

this!" Exhaustion made her shoulders droop and her arms were as heavy as lead. "All because I wanted to dance in the show. I was so pleased you gave me a chance..."

"Exactly!" Glacia Blizzard seemed to be flying, her feet not touching the ice at all. "The funny thing is, you didn't even need to be able to skate. Your unicorn could have done the dance. After all the skates are enchanted – they do all the work."

"Then why did you audition us?" Grace lifted her arms as she was hurled skywards in a sagging pirouette. "Why did we all have to make up a routine for you if it didn't matter how well we could dance?"

"To see who wanted it most, of course," grinned Glacia. "At first I felt certain it was Princess Precious. She's so spoilt and greedy. She was desperate to show off. But, then, I saw you. So loyal and brave – and so fed up of being the clumsy one. I knew you would do anything to prove you could be a perfect princess..."

"You tricked me," said Grace, her knees wobbling as she skated on. "You tricked us all."

"Believe that if you want to," cackled Glacia. She was swirling high above Grace's head now, pulling down a thick grey icy mist. "But the very first moment you saw the skates, you dreamed of wearing them. You wanted to forget Cragland with its hairy yaks and clumpy snowshoes. You longed to prove Cousin Precious wrong. You were desperate to show everyone that you are not a disgrace. You wished with all your heart to be the sort of princess who could make Tall Towers proud. Isn't that what Izumi promised you?"

"Izumi!" As soon as Grace heard her friend's name, she spun around. She remembered Izumi was still in the pavilion. She was with the Ice Maidens, changing their costumes. Grace had to warn her. If Izumi had not been turned to ice, there was still a chance she might be able to get away. Perhaps if she escaped, she could find someone to help.

Grace tried to glide towards the pavilion but the skates pulled her back, looping the loop the other way. "Izumi!" Grace hollered at the top of her lungs.

But, the moment her friend appeared between the pillars, Grace realized she had made a terrible mistake. Now Grace had called for her, Izumi would never escape.

Glacia Blizzard laughed.

"What is it?" Izumi asked. "What's happening?

"Go back inside," yelled Grace.

But, drawn by the magic of the silver

boots, Izumi glanced down at Grace's feet. Instantly, she turned into a frozen statue of solid ice.

CHAPTER TWENTY-ONE
The Endless Dance

"I still don't understand," Grace groaned as she spun helplessly away from her frozen friend. She was so tired, she wanted to lie down right there on the frozen lake and sleep. "Why did you want to turn everyone to ice in the first place? What good will it do you?"

But, even as she asked the question, Grace gasped. The woman skating beside her was growing old before her eyes. In moments, she was no longer Glacia

Blizzard at all, but Miss Wintermore, the wardrobe mistress.

Grace realized she had never seen the two of them together. Only one of them had ever been in the boot room, or out on the ice, or even on the deck of the ship.

"No wonder!" gasped Grace. Glacia and Miss Wintermore were the same person.

"As you see, I am old," said the enchantress. "Old and crooked like the person you know as Miss Wintermore. That is how I must spend my days, trapped inside an ancient, broken body." The elderly witch spun in a circle, whirling three times around Grace. "I get *so* weary being old."

Then suddenly, there she was, young and beautiful once again. As the wrinkles disappeared, Glacia Blizzard's smooth white cheeks and rosy lips reappeared. "My powers are fading. I can only be young in the darkness now," she sighed. "I am doomed to be old in the light of day."

Grace realized it was true. "I've never seen you in the daytime. I mean, I've never seen Glacia Blizzard," she said. She had seen Miss Wintermore many times. "I always thought it odd the rehearsals were so late in the day. You always disappear at the first sign of daylight."

"Each dawn I turn back into frail old Miss Wintermore. I have never been able to stop it happening," said Glacia. "But all that will be different now. At sunrise tomorrow everything will change."

Grace felt a knot of terror twisting in her gut. "What will change?" she asked, knowing that the answer would somehow involve the endless dance she was trapped in and the stone cold figures of every princess in the school.

"Tomorrow is my birthday. I turn one hundred years old at dawn," grinned the witch. "But, thanks to you, I can stay young for ever. I will draw all the energy and life from these beautiful, young princesses. As daylight floods the sky, I will take all the power from their hearts and replace it with chips of ice."

"And what will happen to them then?" asked Grace. Her legs were trembling. She skidded as close to the frozen audience as the skates would allow. Scarlet's raised hand seemed to be reaching out towards her. Even Precious's statue looked more desperate than angry now, as if she had been trying to call out to Grace for help.

"For now, your young friends' hearts are still warm. But soon, like water in a winter pond, the last flicker of life will freeze solid within them," said Glacia. "Frozen for ever, they will remain cold lifeless statues of ice."

"And the teachers?" Grace looked at the motionless figures of stern Flintheart, wise and beautiful Lady DuLac, kind Fairy Godmother Pom in the desperate hope that one of them might move. Might offer some last chance of help...

"It will be the same for them," laughed Glacia. "They will all stay frozen, just as long as you keep dancing through till dawn."

Grace felt a flash if hope. "You mean, if I stop dancing, the spell will be broken."

"Precisely!" Glacia spun around Grace, whipping up a storm of sleet and ice. "But you can't stop dancing, can you?" she laughed. "Not while you are wearing the silver skates. You will dance for all eternity now, my dear."

*

On and on Grace danced, performing difficult turns and twists she would never have dreamed of before tonight. She had no idea how long she had been skating for. It must have been hours.

"I knew you had good stamina," said Glacia, who glided effortlessly beside her, wrapped in a cloak of mist. "I watched you from the pavilion, you know, going round and round the lake with that silly golden chair. You never gave up!"

Grace said nothing. She was so tired her brain felt like scrambled eggs. She would have given anything for the little golden chair right now – so that she could sit down and think. But her feet kept on skating. Far out across the sea, she could see the first pink glow of dawn. She didn't have long. It was up to her to save the entire school – but the only way she could do that was if she could stop the skates from moving. She had tried kicking them off, as she sped across the ice. But that was useless. Izumi had tied the laces tight and the skates fitted so perfectly, they might as well have been frozen to her feet.

"Think," murmured Grace as Glacia Blizzard spun in circles around her head. Stopping dancing had never been a problem for Grace before – usually she was too busy tripping over her own big feet.

"That's it," she whispered. It came to her as clear as a note written on parchment. "I have to be myself. My old self. I have to be good old clumsy Grace."

Almost as soon as she decided it, Grace stumbled a little on the ice.

"Careful!" snapped Glacia, but Grace sped away, filled with new energy.

She jumped and thumped and leapt and

pounded – anything she could do, except be graceful. She leant far too far forward and tipped her head way too far back.

"Stop it!" snarled Glacia.

But Grace closed her eyes and skated backwards at full tilt. "I'm not even looking where I am going," she whooped. "I don't care!" Grace knew if she could just fall over the endless skating would have to stop.

She put her hands over her eyes and spun so fast she had no idea which way she was facing any more. When she looked up, she was so dizzy, she staggered like a newborn yak.

Wham! She hit something hard and cold.

"Precious!" she cried. She had skated full tilt into her cousin's frozen figure at the edge of the ice. "Perfect!"

That did it.

At last, her legs gave way underneath her

and Grace crumpled into a heap on the ice.

She had done it. She had stopped skating
at last.

"Stand up!" snarled Glacia. "Please..." She
was wobbling too now and her legs gave way
beneath her as she sunk down on the ice.
"I suppose you think you're very clever."

"Not clever," said Grace, "just clumsy!"
She was already scrabbling to untie the laces
on the silver skates.

CHAPTER TWENTY-TWO
The Dawn Comes

With one wild kick, the silver skates were gone. They skidded away across the ice.

As soon as they had left her feet, Grace looked up and saw Precious twitch and move above her.

"Hooray!" Grace threw her arms around her cousin's ice-cold knees.

"Get off! What are you doing down there?" spat Precious. Grace had never been so pleased to hear that voice in all her life.

She could see that the other princesses

and the teachers were moving now, yawning and stretching as if they had been asleep for days. Only Izumi, who had been frozen for less time, seemed fully alert. "Look!" she cried, speeding across the lake towards Grace.

Grace turned and saw that Glacia Blizzard was crawling on her knees ... except she wasn't Glacia Blizzard any more. She wasn't even Miss Wintermore. She was a pale, frosty shadow, melting into a pool of water on the ice.

A sudden squawk made Grace turn her head.

"The Ice Maidens," cried Izumi as they looked towards the pavilion. They saw twelve beautiful ice-white birds rise up and fly out through the open door.

"The snow geese," smiled Grace. "Glacia must have enchanted them and turned them into dancers for her show. No wonder they never spoke. They couldn't. They weren't really human at all."

The twelve magnificent birds flew low over her head in a perfect V.

"They don't need to speak now," said Izumi, flinging her arms around Grace's neck. "They are saying thank you to you, that's for sure!"

The geese squawked and Grace laughed. "Head south," she cried as they flew away. "Find somewhere warm for the winter!"

Next thing Grace knew, Scarlet was beside her too. "What happened?" she asked.

"We were turned to ice, but Grace saved us," said Izumi.

Grace blushed. But together they both began to explain everything that they knew. A crowd of princesses gathered around, with Flintheart and Lady DuLac too.

Grace left Izumi talking and tiptoed to

the edge of the group. She had to hop wildly from foot to foot as the ice was freezing cold and, since she had taken off the magic skates, she had nothing to keep her warm but the thin tights from her fairy costume.

All that was left of Glacia Blizzard – or Miss Wintermore – was the pool of cold silvery water. Grace could see the reflection of the fading flames of the torches flickering in it, and also a soft pink light from the sky, growing brighter all the time.

"We're safe," she smiled. "Here comes the dawn!" But as Grace lifted her head to call out to her friends, she saw that Precious had slipped away from the rest of the group. She already had one of the silver skates in her hand and was reaching for the second one too.

"Put them down," cried Grace. She bounded forward but leapt in the air with a yelp of cold as she felt the freezing ice through the stockings on her feet. "Stop her!" she cried.

But everyone was cheering her name and clapping her on the back.

"You're a hero, Grace," they beamed.

"We really are very proud," said Lady DuLac.

"Thank you, but ... sorry to be rude..." Grace dodged past the headmistress, looking desperately for Scarlet and Izumi who were lost somewhere in the crowd. Nobody else seemed to understand what needed to be done.

"We have to stop Precious," she cried, but even her best friends looked confused. Perhaps it was the noise of one hundred princesses cheering all at once.

Then Grace saw them – her big flat snowshoes. They were leaning against the side of the ballet studio where she had left them that very first day it snowed.

"Out of my way!" She pushed aside the twins, who were standing in the studio door, and dived for the home-made shoes.

A moment later, the old tennis rackets were strapped safely to her feet and Grace was off, flying at full speed across the ice.

Precious was on the far side of the lake by now. She was still wearing her own P.P. skates, but had the silver ones tucked tightly under her arm.

"Leave them," said Grace. "You mustn't put them on. They're cursed."

"I don't believe you," Precious spun around. "You just want to keep them yourself. These skates should be mine. I know they should."

She held the boots high above her head. Grace leapt up but, tall as she was, she couldn't reach them.

Precious turned and sped away.

"Stop!" Grace lunged after her. Now she was out on the open lake with plenty of room to manoeuvre, her snowshoes were sliding perfectly.

Thank goodness I am not on skates, she thought. Without an enchantment, she could never skate well enough to catch up with Precious. But the snowshoes were perfect: flat and fast and reliable. Grace had been wearing them all her life, and she was proud to wear them again now.

"This is just like Fish Head Scoot," she panted, imagining that Precious was one of Papa's warriors on the opposite team. All she had to do was mark her closely, swoop down and snatch the fish head – or, in this case, the silver skates.

With a swoosh of ice, she dived towards Precious, skidding on the side of her snowshoes so that one moment she was behind her cousin, the next in front.

She grabbed for the skates, freeing them from Precious's hand. "Got them."

She held the silver skates high in the air for a moment, transfixed by the way they shimmered in the bright pink light of dawn.

But, quickly as she could, she skidded back across the ice towards the startled, staring crowd.

She placed the skates in Lady DuLac's safe hands.

"Promise you'll never let anybody wear them, ever again?" she said.

"I will lock them safely away," said Lady DuLac. "Until we find a way to get rid of them for good."

Grace was a hero. Everywhere she went in school for the next week, people cheered, or curtsied, or patted her on the back.

Even Flintheart took her to one side. "You

are turning into a fine and proper Tall Towers princess," she said. "I know you are not in my class any more, but that does not stop me feeling very proud."

"Thank you," grinned Grace and she found she was pleased to have made Flintheart smile (even if was only for a moment).

"Now go and change your pinafore, Young Majesty. That one has ink on it," the teacher sighed.

Only Precious wouldn't say a word of thanks. She was still sulking and hanging around in the corridor outside Lady DuLac's office.

"I'm worried she might try and steal the silver skates again," Grace told Scarlet and Izumi.

Then, early one morning, she had an idea.

"Come on," she woke her friends. When

they saw the light was on in Lady DuLac's office, they knocked on the door.

"Can we have the skates, please?" asked Grace.

"Have you come up with a way of getting rid of them?" asked the headmistress, unlocking the safe.

"Yes," answered Grace. "I am going to play a game of Fish Head Scoot."

Grace took the skates out on to the middle of the frozen lake and hit them as hard as she could with a big stick. They skidded away across the ice and sank with a plop into a deep fishing hole.

"Nobody will ever be able to reach them down there," she said.

"Certainly not," agreed Scarlet. "This lake is far too deep."

"And a thaw will be on its way soon

anyway," said Izumi. With her usual keen
eye she had spotted a tiny snowdrop peeping
through the ground near the weeping willow
tree. "That means warmer weather must be
coming to Coronet Island."

"Hooray," said Grace. "I can't wait to ride Billy again!"

But there was time for one final snowball fight. Everyone joined in – even Flintheart was seen to throw a snowball. It hit Precious who was sulking under the hedge.

At last Grace was exhausted, and she collapsed, spreading her arms out wide.

Her two best friends flopped down beside her.

"Are we going to make snow fairies?" asked Scarlet

"I think I've had enough of trying to be a fairy," groaned Grace.

"How about we make snow bats instead?" said Izumi.

"Perfect!" grinned Grace.

The three friends laughed as they swooshed their arms up and down, making crazy shapes together in the snow.

Acknowledgements:

I would like to hurl a big soft snowball of thanks for everybody who has made this book possible: my brilliant editor Emily Lamm, Rachel Phillipps for publicity and the rights and sales teams, plus everybody at Scholastic who have worked so hard. To Kim Scott, for her brilliant pictures, of course. Also Pat White and Claire Wilson at RCW. Julia Leonard and Sophie "the Bake-Off" McKenzie for brilliant advice and yummy treats. Also to my family who had to watch me endlessly pretending to skate like a princess in my socks across the slippery kitchen floor ... when they know, full well, what a wobbler on the ice I really am... Thank you all for helping me and Grace have so much fun again!

It's Grace's first term at Tall Towers Princess Academy and she can't wait to make friends, meet her unicorn and learn how to be the perfect princess. If only Grace wasn't the clumsiest pupil that Tall Towers has ever had. . . Can she prove that being a princess is about more than being perfect?

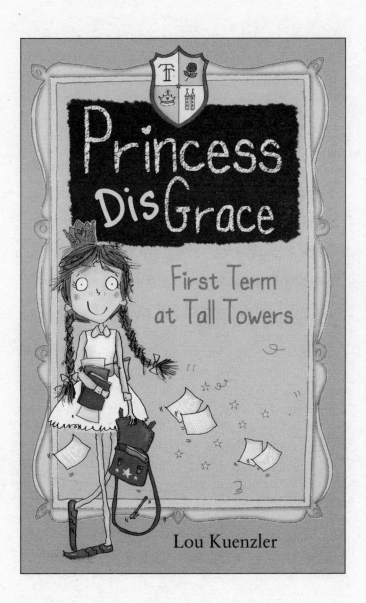

Spring is in the air — and the princesses must perform in the Ballet of the Flowers. If only Grace wasn't so clumsy! But she has other things on her mind — a row with her friends, a mysterious baby unicorn, and rumours that the dragons on Coronet Island aren't extinct after all. . .

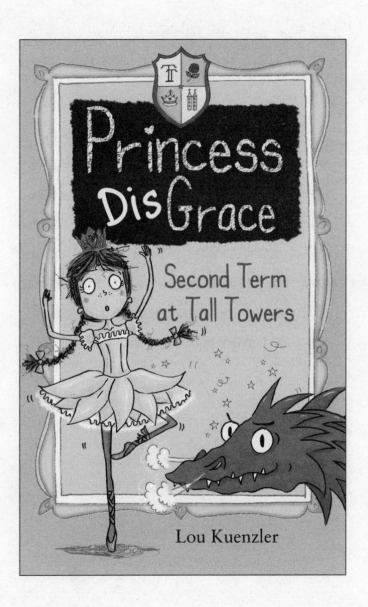

Princess DisGrace

Second Term at Tall Towers

Lou Kuenzler

Summer has come to Tall Towers!
Grace can't wait to start swimming lessons,
especially when she discovers the princesses
will be taught by real mermaids! But their
beautiful young teacher, Waverley, is in trouble.
Only Grace can save her – but time is running
out! Can she solve the mermaid mystery
before it's too late?

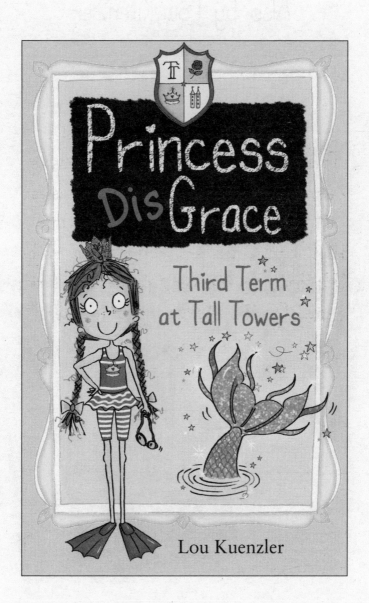

Princess DisGrace

Third Term at Tall Towers

Lou Kuenzler

Also by Lou Kuenzler

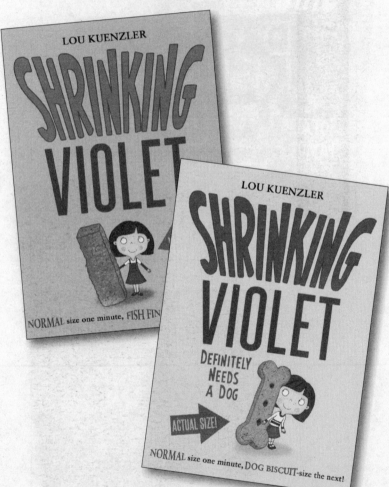

LOU KUENZLER

SHRINKING
VIOLET
IS
TOTALLY
FAMOUS

ACTUAL SIZE!

NORMAL size one minute, LIPST

LOU KUENZLER

SHRINKING
VIOLET
ABSOLUTELY
LOVES
ANCIENT
EGYPT

NORMAL size one minute, MINIATURE-size the next!